RETURN TO TUCKARIMBA

by

AMANDA DOYLE

Harlequin Books

TORONTO • LONDON • NEW YORK • AMSTERDAM • SYDNEY • WINNIPEG

Original hard cover edition published in 1975
by Mills & Boon Limited

SBN 373-01960-2

Harlequin edition published March 1976

Printed in Canada

CHAPTER ONE

WENONA allowed her eyes to travel once more, curiously, over the profile of the man standing just ahead of her in the queue.

She had forgotten her own impatience, and the unstamped letters in her hand, temporarily at least, because there was something about the simple, elderly figure of that man that tugged at the strings of her memory, pulled at them irresistibly, in fact. *Should* she know him? *Did* she know him?

It was one of those tantalizing and uncertain moments which we have all encountered at some time or another – a sense of familiarity with something which reason assures us must be totally unfamiliar, whether it be the curve of a mountain which we recognize, yet have never known; the path of a road, untrodden, yet whose hidden direction we can somehow predict; the planes and hollows of a stranger's face, the composition of features and form, all unfamiliar, yet welding themselves together into a fleeting vision of some past memory, as this man's features now were fusing themselves, before Wenona's doubting eyes, into an image that was at once foreign and yet distractingly nostalgic.

The queue shuffled impatiently.

'Next, please.'

It was almost her turn. Wenona received a small push from behind, to tell her that she was dreaming.

'Sorry.'

She stepped smartly forward to close the gap, and the old man half turned. Again her memory was taunting her, yet she knew she must be wrong. There was no hint of recognition in the faded blue eyes that dwelt for just a moment on her own pale oval face with an impartiality that was convincingly total.

And then the counter clerk solved the whole problem for her in one swift, concise query.

'Yes, Mr. Bunford?'

Ted Bunford! The mailman out at Tucka!

'Bundy,' the children on that run had known him as. Bundy, who had come each week in a rattling old lorry with water-bags flapping from its rusting sides and two spare wheels affixed primly to the top of its peeling cab. They looked as gaudy and improbable as a cocktail hat on the dyed curls of an ageing harlot – an unlikely, yet compelling, combination. The lorry had been crammed with station stores, parcels, bags of sugar and flour, machinery spares, canvas mailbags with stout leather collars and padlocks, tins of groceries, packs of butter in a deep wooden chest, swirling about like fat yellow barges on a pond of melting ice. Bundy's pockets had held not only tobacco wads and cigarettes and papers, but boiled sweets in assorted colourful stripes and peppermints with holes in the middle. Bundy had been the event of the week in that lonely outback area.

The old man was getting coins from the counter, sliding his gnarled brown hand under the grille between himself and the counter-clerk and scooping the money into his cupped palm and from there into his jacket pocket. The dollar notes he counted systematically before folding them carefully and placing them in his wallet. His fingers were shaky but somehow determined. It looked as though it had been a long time since they dealt out tobacco wads and striped bulls'-eyes with the firmness Wenona remembered so well. As indeed it was. A long, long time. An eternity in Wenona's mind, as she groped to recall things that were suddenly more important than plugs of tobacco and sticky boiled sweets. Her brain, trembling on the brink of remembrance, somehow could

6

not bridge the gap of time. Her failure to do so made her want to cry.

Now Bundy was turning away, walking slowly out of the building. Out of her groping recollections.

Wenona followed, her place in the queue, her unposted letters, forgotten.

'Mr. Bunford? Mr. Bunford? Bundy?'

The old man stopped as she used the diminutive, his faded eyes sharpening.

'It *is* Mr. Bunford? From – from Tuckarimba?'

'Yeah, that's right, miss. An' *you* called me *Bundy*.' He made it sound like a presumption.

Wenona flushed.

'Yes, I did. I – we used to call you that. I hope you didn't mind, but I had to stop you somehow.' She took a breath. 'I'm from Tuckarimba myself, or used to be. Wenona. Maybe you remember? Fat and short, with fair plaits? I wore glasses then, too.'

'Wenona? Yer don't mean *Nonie*?' He stared, incredulous now. 'Well, skin the flamin' lizards if it isn't little Nonie Dermot!'

'Nonie Gotthart. My – my mother married again. I took my stepfather's name.'

'Yeah? Well, I reckon yer mother did the right thing there, eh.' The old man grunted agreement with his own statement. He was still gazing at her in some amazement. 'S'truth, yer growed some, didn't yer, Nonie? Who'd 'ave thought that that tubby little sheila 'ud turn into a bee-oot-iful long-legged young dame like you? Except, maybe, y're a bit *too* skinny now, I reckon. Yer've gone the other way now, see. Too thin.' He continued his frank assessment.

They stood there together on the pavement, looking at each other, with the rows of Norfolk Island pines behind them, and the beach wall behind those, and then the sand and the pounding, white-frothed breakers. The wind

7

soughed gently through the needled foliage. It ruffled Mr. Bunford's white locks, and lifted Wenona's long blonde tresses, whipping them across her pale cheeks.

'Look, Bundy, could you spare time for a cup of coffee – or even a beer, maybe?'

'I reckon I could. It ain't every day I meet someone from the old life.' He shuffled willingly along at her side, and she matched her steps to his.

When they stopped, it was to sit down at an outdoor café, with small tables set back from the pavement. Wenona chose coffee, and bought Bundy the promised schooner.

'Have you been back, Bundy? How long is it since you left? How long have you been in Sydney, and whatever are you doing *here*? You're the last person I'd ever have expected to see, here on the corso at Manly!'

The old man put down his beer and grinned.

'Well, you're a bit of a surprise yerself, come ter that, Nonie.' He wiped the froth off his tobacco-stained moustache with the back of his hand. 'I've been here a good long time now, as it happens. Ten years, about. And – let's see. You were only eight when your dad – when you – er – left. And I was there at Tucka a good five years after that, so that makes you—?'

'I'm twenty-three.'

'Funny, that. An' I'm seventy-six.' He sighed. 'Little Nonie Dermot, twenty-three.'

'Gotthart.'

'Eh?'

'Gotthart. Nonie *Gotthart*. My mother married again. Remember, I've already told you? And I took my step-father's surname.' She paused. 'I've actually got a little sister, too, Bundy – a half-sister, from my mother's second marriage. Pru is eight herself now – just about the age I was when I left Tuckarimba.'

'That's nice. A young sister, eh? And is her – is yer

8

stepfather a decent bloke, then, Nonie?'

'He was a darling,' Wenona told him warmly. 'He's dead now, Bundy,' she added without embarrassment, 'but he was the very best stepfather a girl could have or wish for.'

'Well, yer ma deserved that, at the very least. She deserved a break. Where is she now, yer mother, Nonie?'

'She died, Bundy, when Pru was born – no, don't look like that, of course you had to ask. The doctor said she shouldn't have had such a late child, after all she'd been through. It didn't work out for her, I'm afraid, that's all.'

She swallowed, looked away so that he wouldn't see the quick tears that, even after all this time, could spring to her eyes so easily when she remembered her mother – so gentle, and kind, patient and happy, and yet always with a brooding sort of sadness tucked away behind the cheerfulness, a lurking wistfulness, almost as if she had known that she was never going to hold the child that she was carrying.

'I'm sorry, Nonie.' The old chap was gruff. 'Like I said, she deserved better luck than that. It took it out of 'er, that whole business about yer dad. She kept 'er head up, too, right ter the day she left. Defended 'im right, left, 'n centre, but I'll bet it took it out of 'er, more than she'd ever 'ave admitted. Reckon we all liked yer mother, Nonie. We admired 'er, see. That's why we all went along with 'er about yer father's accident. Well, it *could* 'ave been one, couldn't it? I mean, there was no *note* or anything like that.'

A coldness feathered over Wenona's skin. Her eyes were beginning to widen.

'You mean—?' She hesitated, schooled herself to calmness as the implication of what he had said was borne in upon her.

She made herself look at him with candour.

'I never knew that there was anything – I never knew exactly how my father died, except that he was drowned.'

'Well, that's all that *anyone* knew, but there was plenty of speculation.' Mr. Bunford scratched his ear uncomfortably. 'I should know at my age when ter keep my big mouth shut, shouldn't I?'

'No, it doesn't matter. Truly, Bundy.' Wenona shrugged a little ruefully. 'The people most concerned are often the last to hear these things, I realize that quite well. I've learned to be realistic about things, Bundy – I've had to be, you see, with Pru to bring up on my own. I've had to look facts in the face, even unpalatable ones, and I think I've realized all along that my father couldn't have been a very strong or dependable character. But he was kind – good fun, *great* fun. He loved me.'

' 'E was a – a *whimsical* sort of cove, yer dad. A bit of a dreamer, Nonie. Providence – the hard "outback" sort of Providence, I mean – ain't all that kind ter dreamers, yer know. It's the hard-bitten sort that make a go of it out there. Floods an' bush-fires an' droughts an' dust-storms aren't fer dreamin' fellers like yer dad.'

She smiled, gently.

'I know. I think I realized that even then, young and all as I was. And yet all my memories – my *happiest* memories – are of Tuckarimba. My – I suppose one could say that my father was a failure, Bundy? And yet, at Tuckarimba, even that didn't seem to matter, not to a child anyway. They were idyllic days, safe and secure, filled with sunshine and warmth and laughter, and the interest and variety of the changing country scene. I can think of no better background for a small child to grow up with.'

'Huh. It ain't all beer and skittles, like *you* make it seem.' But even Bundy sounded unconvinced, nostalgic.

She sighed, half-closed her eyes.

'I've often wondered what happened to it all, after we left.'

'D'yer really want ter know?' The old man hesitated. 'Reckon I don't want ter shoot down any more of them ideas of yours.'

'Do you know?'

'Reckon the bank had a bond on the place when yer dad died, Nonie.'

'So that was why we never had any money! I was too young to understand, but looking back I'd have guessed, anyway, if I'd really thought about it. I realize now what a struggle it must have been for Mum, from the time we left right up to when she married Stroud Gotthart. What *did* happen to it, then?'

'The Tintoola Pastoral Company took it off the bank, and put in a manager. It's a good property, yer know, but the drought years hit 'em pretty hard right from the word go.'

'Who are the Tin – whatever it was you said?'

The old mailman looked askance at what he obviously considered a display of abysmal ignorance.

'The Lomax outfit. Strings of stations further north – west, too. In the end it got so bad that Jacey Lomax himself came down ter lick things inter shape.'

'Jacey Lomax? He'd be the – er – the head?'

'Yeah, the boss uv the works. Young, tough, full uv drive like 'is dad was before 'im. I guess wherever Jacey goes 'e gets things done, and that's what 'e did at Tuckarimba too. In fact, 'e fell in love with the place an' stayed. Funny ter think of a *Lomax* fallin' fer a bit of real fancy country like Tucka. They're all north coves, that lot – plains-'n-ranges, don't-fence-me-in sort of fellers – but no, Jacey fell smack in love with Tuckarimba, I reckon. It's a small place by *their* standards, just thirty odd thousand acres, but it got under 'is skin, see. Once 'e'd got it how 'e wanted it, 'e found 'e didn't want ter leave it.'

'And he's there now?'

'Yep, 'e is. They say 'e's away a lot, of course. Flies around visitin' the other stations, takin' a dekko at what's goin' on, but Tucka's 'is base.'.

Mr. Bunford alias Bundy drained the dregs from his schooner, took out a large grey handkerchief and passed it along his moustache from one side of his mouth to the other.

Wenona finished her own coffee in silence, trying idly to imagine what the place would be like now – now that this Jacey Lomax had 'licked it into shape'.

'Funny me runnin' inter you like this, Nonie,' the ex-mailman mused pensively. 'I 'aven't seen so much as a cat's whisker of the folk from Tucka fer years, and then in two days I do a double. 'Ad a letter from Mickey Doolan – 'e used ter be at the store, but I doubt if you'd remember Mickey. Well, Mick's got a little show of 'is own now, out at Innamincka, an' 'e went ter see 'is aunt at Tucka a coupla days ago, an' 'e happened ter mention Tuck-arimba. And then I run inter you. That's what I mean by funny.'

'What did he say?' Wenona leaned forward eagerly.

'Said the old homestead's fer sale.'

'Sale! You mean Tuckarimba? Our old house?'

That hurt, somehow. It didn't add up, either, with the fact that Jacey Lomax had fallen in love with the place. Nonie had found herself harbouring quite a soft spot for the great Jacey Lomax for having the good sense to fall in love with a place like Tuckarimba, in spite of the dimensions of all his other interests. It showed him to be a man of soul and sensitivity. But now, to want to *sell* it—

'Are you sure?' she asked Bundy dubiously. 'Sure you've got it right, I mean?'

'Most certainly I'm sure. Dinkum sure. It's only the

house an' the orchard 'e's sellin', because it's right at the town end of the property, as yer know, an' Jacey didn't like the site.'

'Didn't like the *site*!' Her opinion of Jacey Lomax and his soul and sensitivity were altering fast! 'Why, it's a beautiful site. A – a *heavenly* site!'

'Well, Jacey don't hold your views on that, apparently. Too shut in, down there on the creek flat. I *told* yer Jacey's lot are don't-fence-me-in fellers. 'E's built 'imself a ruddy great new homestead further up the river, where 'e can look right down the valley an' see what's goin' on, Mick says.'

'The lord of all he surveys?' she broke in, and was amazed at her own waspishness.

'Yeah, that's Jacey,' agreed the old man imperturbably, unaware of her sarcasm. 'Fer a while there was an overseer in the old place, but now Jacey's wantin' ter get quit of it. Now 'e's livin' there 'e doesn't need a full-time overseer. He's the sort that likes ter keep the tabs on things 'imself, if 'e can, see. Mickey says 'e shoved in ten acres of creek flat along with it, with the idea that someone might make a market garden out of it, being at the town end of the run, yer see.'

Wenona found it all hard to believe. That anyone could *prefer* another site! That anyone could *want* to be quit of it!

It was difficult to visualize the old homestead, admittedly in an advanced state of antiquity, cut off from the rest of the place to which it had always belonged for so many years. Cut off. *Fenced* off, along with a mere ten puny acres. *Spurned.*

It was an insult! And they called him a don't-fence-me-in feller!

'Are you certain?' she persisted, but very feebly, because she now knew exactly the sort of hands into which poor old Tuckarimba had fallen.

13

'Dead certain. Mickey said 'e took a run out, and there's even a great big "For Sale" notice stuck on a pole near the old wattle tree.'

'The wattle tree! You used to stop the mail-lorry right beside it, Bundy!'

'That's the one. A big white board with black letterin', Mick said. Said 'e felt quite sad ter see it, but times change, I reckon.' He stood up, and Wenona scraped her own chair back too. 'Well, Nonie, it's been good ter meet yer like this, talkin' about old times an' all that.'

'Yes, Bundy,' she agreed. 'You live here now, in Manly?'

'With Florrie, me sister. She's me youngest sister, like. Never got 'erself hitched. There was a bloke once – a shearer – out on the Paroo—' he gestured vaguely.

'It's nice that you've got each other now, though. Maybe I'll see you around, Bundy. We must keep in touch, after this.'

'Yeah, that's right, Nonie. We'll keep in touch. Thanks fer the beer, then.' He clasped her hand for a brief moment. 'S'long, Nonie.'

'So long, Bundy. See you around,' replied Wenona automatically, but already she had the strangest feeling that she wasn't going to *be* around – not here in Manly, anyway. Already she had a suspicion that she knew just what the inevitable outcome of this conversation was going to be.

And why not? she asked herself cautiously, as she walked slowly back to the room which she and Pru shared together. They not only shared the room with each other, but the bathroom and kitchen facilities with the other bedroom-occupiers in the same building. What sort of existence was *that* for Pru, compared with the freedom of a rambling corridor of rooms to themselves, and the chance to shout and sing and jump and skip out there at Tuckarimba, where there were no other people to keep on telling her to be quiet, keep down her voice, shut the door, stay on her own stair, pull down the blind, leave the flower-beds alone.

Wenona let herself into the building, glanced at her watch. Soon Pru would be home from school.

She took off her jacket, went through to the shared kitchenette, and began to clear the crumbs off the table. The breadknife looked as if someone had spread jam with it and then put it straight back on the board. It wasn't *her* breadknife. Not even *her* crumbs.

Strange that such a tiny, irritating detail as that could be responsible for a whole chain of decisions, a whole string of events, but it was!

Wenona ran the knife under the hot tap, her mind busy with the obstacles, tackling them in turn, eliminating them one by one. As her fingers went on cutting the bread for Pru's tea, she was almost unaware of her own actions, so taken up was she with her thoughts.

What sort of a life was this for Pru? she asked herself again. Coming home each day to the same dingy place in the same dingy back street, the same dull routine, the same tedious restrictions? And what about Wenona herself? Wenona, the part-time – part-time *what*? How could she accurately describe herself, or this mad life she led? Part-time sign-writer, because she had taken a course in it once; part-time picture-framer, because it was something she could do right here, at one end of the bed-sitting room while she was looking after Pru, and a notice in the local newsagent's window occasionally put custom her way; part-time typer of envelopes, because the money was good even if her typing wasn't; part-time cleaner, because in return for doing out the landlady's own flat, which took up the whole of the top floor, she was 'let off' four dollars a week in rent; part-time gardener, because she got another two dollars off for keeping the path to the main front door free of weeds. Part-time jack-of-all-trades, and master of absolutely *none* of them, that's what she was, and she was thoroughly tired of the whole set-up! Where was it getting either herself or Pru? Precisely nowhere!

She had three thousand dollars saved.

Well, nearly, if you included the bit which Stroud had left that wasn't actually in trust for Pru when she grew up. If you added that on to what she already had herself, it was nearly three thousand.

Surely that would be enough for a down-payment, a loan or something, to get that crumbling, *dear* old homestead that the Lomax man didn't want? The orchard could be productive almost straight away. She could maybe bottle fruit, too, and sell home-made jam, and that lovely alluvial soil down on the creek flats would grow fabulous vegetables. She might even try things like mushrooms and asparagus, that needed special beds and temperatures. She had no idea just *what* they needed, but she could soon read it up and apply the knowledge she had gleaned, like she had done with the picture-framing. And all the time she was doing these things, there'd be the sunshine, the open air, the scent of the wattle tree, the sound of bees in the gum-blossoms, the peace and variety and freedom that were Tuckarimba's. They would be hers and Pru's, to enjoy as freely as they pleased.

It took two days to get away.

Wenona was quite surprised that it had taken even that, so determined was she upon her new course of action, but in the end there had been an alarming number of things to which to attend.

She had had to pay the landlady right up to the end of the month in lieu. That had been a bit of a setback, but she supposed it was really fair enough. Tenants weren't supposed to go haring off into the blue at a moment's notice, after all – but it would be worth it in the end, because if she didn't get out to Tuckarimba quickly, someone else might see the 'For Sale' notice and get there first, and that would be too unbearable even to contemplate, now that her mind was made up.

Next, she had had to transfer her account to the bank at Tucka. The manager of the local branch had looked dubious when she had explained just why, but he had shaken her hand in rather grave dismissal after agreeing to her request, and had even wished her well, with a doubtful smile on his lips. Wenona had been glad that she had got around him so easily. It had been somewhat chastening to have to stand there and listen to his paternal lecture on the inadvisability of rash and impulsive decisions, but she had done so knowing that she had no intention of being talked out of anything.

Then there had been Pru's teacher to see, and initial inquiries as to the relative merits of correspondence courses and lessons at small country schools.

After all that, travelling arrangements, and finally, packing up. The packing didn't take long, because even between them there was not much to pack. Wenona wrapped her mother's old photographs and pictures and other simple trinkets in tissue, tenderly, and then in more brown paper, before laying them carefully in the big trunk which she would send by train to Tucka railway station. She could collect the trunk at the other end, once she knew what her movements would be, and where they would be staying.

They themselves were going by plane. Expensive, yes, but again there was this urgent need for haste, and therefore Wenona felt such untoward extravagance was warranted.

Strange to think that before very long these small, humble treasures of her mother's would be back on the shelves they had known long ago. It all seemed oddly appropriate, that. It helped Wenona to believe in what she was doing. It made her more certain that it was the correct – the only – thing. Tuckarimba, fenced off together with its little river plot, spurned and unwanted by the big Lomax overlord, would know itself to be loved and needed and remembered. It would come alive again, and with its revitalization would come the rediscovery of some of that same happiness and sense of belonging which Wenona, as a child, had experienced there. And this time Pru, too, would have her share.

In the plane she was still preoccupied, exhausted, now, too. She flopped back, thinking. Beside her, Pru's thin brown legs were swinging, her sandalled feet not reaching the floor of the aircraft as the safety-belt held her small, cotton-frocked body against the back of the seat. Her mouse-brown hair stuck out in fine spikes, cropped short, and she peeped excitedly out of the window with wide-set eyes. They were peat-brown in colour, tilting at the outer corners in a way that gave her animated face a slightly startled, pixie look. They were her mother's eyes, and unlike Wenona's own. Hers were her father's, she supposed – Irish eyes, deep lake-blue, with thick black fringes. Eyes that could sulk and brood like descending mist on a lough; eyes that could storm with all the dark threat of a Connemara mountain raincloud; eyes that could sparkle and dance as mischievously as the dappled waters of Killarney itself. Dermot's eyes. Dermot, 'the free one'.

Dermot, the dreamer, more like, she corrected herself practically. Poor Dermot. Poor Father.

No one there would know that she was his daughter, and she didn't intend that they should – not until she had 'made good', as she meant to do. It wasn't that she wanted to *deny* him – no one understood or forgave human failings better than she did herself, but in the meantime, for Pru's sake, things had better remain as they were. Prue had never known about Dermot, and her

mother's 'other life'. It had seemed terribly important, at
the time, that they should be a complete family. Wenona
had been too young to take part in the decision that
changed her surname to that of her stepfather, but she
had loved Stroud Gotthart, and she hadn't minded in the
least. Later, after her mother's tragic death, it was with
his tacit agreement that she had allowed Pru to grow up
thinking from the very start that she and Wenona were
full sisters, and not merely half-ones. Wenona, after all,
was the only female influence in little Pru's life, now that
her mother had gone. It seemed imperative that the relationship would appear total, and indeed Wenona could
almost have believed that Stroud *was* her own father,
because that was the way he had always acted, instinctively and irreproachably.

Pru didn't know about Tuckarimba, either. She had
never even heard of it until two days ago, when Wenona
had mentioned it for the first time, taking her quite by
surprise.

Pru was now wriggling with anticipation, her thin
fingers laced through the harness of the seat-belt as she
edged nearer the glass to peer down over the silver wing-
tip.

'What'll it be like, do you suppose, Nonie?'

'What, darling?'

'What'll it be like, Tucka?'

'You mean the town itself? Oh, just a tiny little place, a
country township. It'll probably have a park where you
can play amongst the trees when we go in to sell our
vegetables and fruit. And a railway. And some shops, and
a sprinkling of houses. From up here I should think it will
look like a tiny toy village, don't you? Everything looks so
small from up here. Those trees down there are just like
little dabs of plasticine, see, and that thin brown ribbon is
really a big, wide river.'

The plane droned on, and Wenona let her head fall

back against the seat again. How weary she was! And yet it was a merely physical weariness, because of all the organizing she had had to do in order to get them both away. There was no Stroud now, to do the things a man normally took care of, like tickets and travel and trunks. There hadn't been Stroud for years, really. Not for years and years. When Wenona thought seriously about the constancy of her struggle to support herself and Pru, to be father and mother and breadwinner combined, she wasn't altogether surprised at her physical state. Mentally, she had coaxed herself into a sort of wooden torpor – an if-I-can-get-through-today-I-can-get-through-tomorrow sort of attitude that had not permitted her to think too broadly of her situation, or too far ahead. That, she told herself now, was how she had managed to cope, how she had succeeded in being a stumbling and not very efficient jack-of-all-trades who yet achieved the daily tasks successfully enough to keep herself and Pru adequately clothed and fed.

Now she was for once allowing her imagination the luxury of a free run. In her mind's eye she could visualize the new Tuckarimba that she was going to make, could smell the blossoms on the fruit trees, see the boughs sagging under their load of warm ripe fruits. Down nearer the creek she would have rows of tomatoes, neatly staked; trellises of beans; melon vines on the rampage, with their pretty white and orange flowers; pumpkins and artichokes and cool green cucumbers.

She would need to get a suitable vehicle, too, to transport her produce. One of those commercial vans, probably, with double doors at the back that would open up so that she could slide things in without squashing them.

She'd think about school for Pru once they had settled in. Daily attendance along with children would probably be preferable to correspondence lessons. It would provide companionship, a little discipline, while allowing Pru the freedom to run wild at Tuckarimba itself – something the poor scrap had never been able to do in the whole of her miserably confined eight years.

'That's it, Nonie! Look! And it's not a little toy town at all. It's a *big* one!'

It was, too. Tucka township was much, much larger than it had been in her day. It had 'arrived', no doubt about it.

As the plane banked low she saw that it now sprawled extensively over the wedge of land between the two rivers that gave Tuckarimba Station its name – 'the joining of the creeks'. Wide streets were planted with oily-leafed kurrajongs that glistened in the sun. Clusters of cedar and willow and soaring heaven-trees were where the tiny park had been. Now she could see an S-shaped swimming-pool, spraying fountains, an orange-tiled pavilion, and what was in all probability a golf-course. The houses, the wide, shaded streets, stretched endlessly, broken by green plots of lawn and bright splashes of colour that were flower gardens and shrubberies. To the left, right out on the fringe, were the sale-yards, silos, railhead, air-strip that characterized all country towns of this sort.

Tucka was almost a city. There would be plenty of demand for fresh garden produce if she worked things properly, got the right contacts. There was obviously a large, busy population, too, compared with the handful of people in her own childhood, and no one would ever connect a too-thin, too-pale, tall young blonde woman called Wenona Gotthart with the podgy, brown, bespectacled eight-year-old Nonie Dermot, if they remembered the latter at all. Besides, Nonie Dermot had been an only child, and here was the young Miss Gotthart with a sister as well – yes, my dear, they've just bought the market garden, the new people – and the old Tuckarimba homestead along with it – quite a pleasant young woman – city, of course, but still – and the sister's a dear little thing with spiky fine hair and a face like an elf.

Wenona's lips twitched. She unfastened Pru's seat-belt and her own, and gathered their bits and pieces together before following the other passengers from the plane.

On the way in from the air-strip Pru chattered incessantly.

'Oh, look, Nonie, there's the park. Swings and everything, see, and a slippery-slide, a roundabout, a hurdy-gurdy thing – and look at that fountain – oh, isn't it *beautiful*, water coming right out of the fish's mouth – do you think he's supposed to be a dolphin, Nonie? – he *looks* a bit like a dolphin, don't you think – he's smiling, and they do smile, dolphins, don't they? I love Tucka, don't you, Nonie? Don't you think it's just *beaut*? *I* think it's a gorgeous place.'

Wenona booked in at one of the better hotels, and when they had washed and brushed up and had taken some afternoon tea, she took Pru out and found a garage that hired out self-drive cars. There should just be time to reach Tuckarimba before darkness came. She wanted to read that sale-board, see in whose hands the transfer of the property had been placed. It was sure to be a local agent, either a stock and station firm, or a solicitor. Whoever it was, she would see him first thing in the morning, and start proceedings to acquire the place. Wenona could hardly wait.

She chose the bigger, better car. It was important to keep up appearances, wasn't it? Just for the present, they must seem to have some 'substance' behind them, some-*financial* 'substance', that is. Where business deals were concerned, you had to think of all these things.

She put her foot down impatiently on the accelerator, and they sped along, bouncing over the corrugated road, leaving a flurrying dust-trail behind them. Memories nudged her at every turn. Yes, she remembered that clump of wilgas, and the signpost nailed to that old yellow box-tree. And here was the wooden bridge over the meeting-place of the creeks – the Boogillgar to the right, and Whalebone Creek to the left.

She took the left fork, along the narrower track flanked by silvery willows, watched over by lofty paperbarks, around the corner that was called Catfish Bend. Ahead, upstream, were the serrated outlines of the rocks that gave the creek its name. Limestone outcrops, smoothed by wind and water, they spanned the creek from one bank to the other in an oblique arc like the vertebrae of a beached whale-corpse. How many times hadn't she leaped gleefully from stone to stone, from one bank to the other, throwing pebbles and sticks into the hurrying channels that rushed amongst the rocks and eventually merged with the slowly frothing pool below!

Another bend, and they would see Tuckarimba.

She bit back the words which she had almost spoken aloud. Pru must not guess that she, too, was not a stranger to this track.

'Do you think we're nearly there, Nonie?' Pru sounded a little anxious. 'It's beginning to get quite dark. The lady at the hotel said it gets dark awfully quickly out here in the country.'

'Not to worry, poppet. It can't be far now. I've been measuring the miles on the speedo, you see. And I've got a torch. We won't stay long. Once we see who I have to contact tomorrow, we'll go back to town and have a proper meal. You'd like that, wouldn't you? We can come back in the daytime to see it all properly. Are you tired?'

'M'm, I am, aren't you? All that packing. I hate packing, don't you, Nonie? I hope we never have to move again, not ever, once we get our very own house like you said we will. I'm longing to get into it, and I won't have that narky old Mrs. Beeston telling me to "keep my voice

23

down" all the time, and "shut that door", and "just look at your sandals, they're *covered* in sand, you've brought in half the *beach!*" '

Wenona couldn't help smiling. Pru was a born mimic, and could imitate the landlady's falsetto carpings to perfection. It was naughty, though, and to be discouraged. Wenona would have checked her for it, but she felt too keyed up, right now, to bother. It couldn't matter, anyway. Not *now*!

As the car rounded the bend and crested the brow of the hill, she braked, and pulled in at the side of the road.

'Look, Pru, that's – that must be it, down there. You can see the roof through the trees, and the creek looping around behind.'

'That big place, Nonie? Right up the far end, with the hills just behind it? I don't see any creek, though. I mean, it's way *above* the creek. But isn't it huge? Quite fabulous!'

Wenona swallowed in dismay. She had only just spied the outline that Pru had been looking at, away in the distance – the outline of a great long homestead, poised in a magnificent position that commanded a view of the entire valley.

The new Tuckarimba, tucked into a fold in the hills, sheltered from the elements, remote from the public highway beneath, appeared as secluded and mysterious in this hushed bush twilight as a Tibetan monastery.

'I don't mean up there, I mean down here, right beneath us. See?'

'Oh, yes, I see. What a dear old house, Nonie! It's got fingers of roof going out in all directions, hasn't it? It looks all muddled and wobbly, as if it didn't know which way to grow next. Oh, Nonie, I love it already! Let's go down and see it closer.'

'Yes, let's.' Wenona's voice was suddenly husky. She

24

started the engine again, and took the car down to the creek flats, slowly, savouring every moment of this home-coming of hers.

It was like a dream, and yet the poignant reality of it sent delicious tremors through her thin, weary frame. She was here! She had made it! Nonie had come home to Tuckarimba – and, this time, so had Pru!

And then, as the homestead came properly into view, right on the level of the creek-flat where the car was now cruising slowly along, Nonie saw that something wasn't quite as she had expected it to be. Lights were on in that squat, sprawling old house, and even as she slowed to a halt and stepped out, another light blinked on, winking out at her like a warning signal.

It wasn't empty! The house wasn't empty!

Unreasoning panic gripped her throat. Something of her urgency reached out to little Pru, skipping along at her side.

'What is it, Nonie? What's the matter?'

She put out her hand, and Nonie grasped it, dragging her sister along in haste.

'I don't know. Perhaps it's just a caretaker, but perhaps it's – it's been – sold. Perhaps we're too late. Quickly, darling, hurry. Let's see if we can see the notice-board. There's a big notice that says it's for sale.'

But there wasn't. Not now. Playing her torch over the ground near the wattle tree, Nonie could see where the hoarding had been. But now there was nothing. Nothing at all.

'It's not there!' Pru's voice was a thin wail.

'No, it's not.'

When Pru began to whimper, Nonie turned and gave her a savage little shake.

'If – you – dare – to – cry, Pru,' she said, very slowly, emphatically, in a strangely strangled voice that held an unfamiliar note of desperation – 'If you dare to cry *now*,

Pru, I'll – I'll *whip* you, so help me, I will!'

'Oh, no, you won't!' A voice spoke from the shadows behind them. It came with a suddenness, a severity, that sent the two of them into each other's arms, clinging together in fright.

'Oh, no, you won't. You'll do no such thing while *I'm* around to witness it, my impetuous young madam! And you don't know much about children, either, if you can't tell that that kid's almost out on her feet, plain tuckered out.'

'Who are you?'

Wenona disengaged herself from Pru's skinny, clinging arms with as much dignity as she could muster, and gazed at the tall, emerging figure of the man who stepped out from the trees behind them. He was leading a horse by the reins. He loomed near her in the dusk, and the horse's hooves crackled on the dried, fallen leaves as it followed its master haltingly, stopping obediently when he did, a few feet from Wenona herself. His broad-shouldered outline was near enough to seem menacing, towering over her in the gathering darkness.

Nonie took a grip on herself. She wasn't the nervous sort, she told herself firmly.

'Who are you?' she asked again, cursing her voice for its betraying tremor, because already she thought she knew!

CHAPTER TWO

'Jason Lomax. What are you doing here?'

'Not—? Not *Jacey* Lomax?' Her confidence ebbed immediately as her worst fears were confirmed.

'Jason Lomax. My initials happen to be J. C., certainly. That's why my friends call me Jacey,' he informed her in a forbidding tone that said *she* wasn't one of those friends, or likely to be! 'You are trespassing,' he added coldly.

'Inspecting a property that's up for sale can hardly be termed trespassing,' she retorted, matching the man's chilly tones.

'You mean the house?' He jerked his head towards the shadowed bulk of the sprawling buildings.

He had taken off the wide-brimmed felt hat that he had been wearing, and now he was twirling it between his fingers, watching her in the dwindling light of dusk. The horse, whose reins were looped carelessly over his arm, nuzzled gently at his back, with soft, snuffling noises.

'Yes, the house.' She was more relaxed now. 'I'd like to buy it.'

'I'm sorry, but that's not possible.' He didn't sound very sorry, though – merely casual, in a definite sort of way.

'It's not *sold*?' Her heart sank.

'No, but it's not for sale, either. So far as you are concerned, there's relatively little difference.'

'But it was. It *was* for sale?' Her voice rose, in spite of all her efforts to appear calm. 'There was a big sale notice, right there by the wattle tree. I saw where it was. The stand itself is there yet.'

'The stand, but not the notice.' He sounded maddeningly indifferent.

'But why?'

'I've changed my mind in the meantime,' he informed her discouragingly, in a voice that also told her clearly that he did not consider his reasons to be any business of hers.

'In the – meantime.' Nonie brightened, hope reviving. 'Does that mean that you *will* be selling it?'

'It means I may,' he returned brusquely. 'Some time,' he emphasized, as if aware of the need to quell her newly springing optimism.

'Then I'll stay around, Mr. Lomax. I've – I've come a long way to get this house.'

'In that case, it would be unfair to mislead you, Miss—?'

'Gotthart, Wenona Gotthart. This is my sister Pru.'

'It's not worth waiting for, Miss Gotthart.' He chucked Pru under the chin with long brown fingers. 'It could be a fair time.'

'It's worth it to me.' There were tears in her voice, in her eyes too, just a little. 'It's worth it to *me*. We've come a – a very long way, but I can wait. If you'll just give me the first chance of it, when you sell?'

'It could be years.'

'Years?' She was startled at the way he'd said the word. He had made it sound like forever, an infinity, eternity.

'Well, a couple, anyway. On the other hand, I might put it on the market again fairly soon. It depends very much on several contingencies of a personal nature.'

'Oh, I see.' He obviously was not going to elaborate upon what the contingencies were. 'Well—' she squared her shoulders, reached for Pru's hand – 'I can wait, Mr. Lomax. I'll stick around.'

The man was peering at her intently. His face, above hers, was darkly tanned, merging into the night itself. It was a long face, square-jawed, heavy-browed, that was all that she could tell. She couldn't see his expression at all.

In a way that was a comfort, because it meant that he couldn't see hers, either!

'I don't think I would stick around, if I were you,' he advised her more gently. 'I think the wisest course where you are concerned would be to go home.'

Home? Home is where the heart is, Mr. Lomax, or didn't you know?

'We don't – er – have a home, exactly, just at the moment.' Her voice faltered a little, uncertainly, as she debated with herself as to how much she should tell him. 'But I'll stay in town, and you can contact me when it becomes available. Who is your man of business?'

'The Tintoola estate office is in the main street. You can hardly miss it.' His tone was dry.

'Oh, I see. Well, when I – when we find somewhere permanent to stay, I'll let them know, so that they can contact me.'

'Don't bank on it.'

'I've learned never to bank on anything, Mr. Lomax,' she retorted, stiltedly, because that was just what she *had* done, wasn't it! 'Come, Pru.'

She turned away stumblingly towards the car, and the man put his hat on his head once again, and began to lead the horse back in amongst the trees. She could hear them crashing through the scrub together.

Nonie put Pru into the car, and got in herself. When she had closed her door, she put her hands on the steering-wheel, without attempting to start the engine. Then she put her head forward and rested her forehead against her hands. Sitting there, slumped against the wheel, she tried to get a grip of herself. She must get herself in hand, overwhelming though the disappointment was. Maybe things would work out in the end. Maybe he'd put the house up again quite soon. She'd need to find a job, and lodgings. They couldn't stay in that expensive hotel—

'Move over.'

'What?'

She looked up, dazed. Her mind was almost too weary to alter course and take in the fact that the man was back.

He had her door open, and was leaning into the car.

'Move over. Hop into the back, young 'un, and give your big sister some room.'

'What are you doing?' Nonie gazed at him blankly.

'Driving you back to town, what else?' He sounded abrupt, impatient.

'You're doing no such thing.'

'Like to bet?' Already his bulk was forcing her to shift grudgingly from her position at the wheel.

'I'm perfectly capable of driving myself, thanks.'

'That's debatable. I don't think you are.'

'I am!'

His eyes narrowed, glinted dangerously.

'You're damn near snapping point, if you ask me. The signs are all there, and I've no intention of having a hysterical female on either my property or my conscience. Besides, your kid sister wants to get home to bed, and I'll get her there quicker than you will.'

There was no point in arguing. Nonie could see that he was not in the mood to have his decisions disputed. Probably no one *ever* disputed decisions that were made by Jacey Lomax. They wouldn't dare. He was the kind who'd always have an improbable ace tucked up his sleeve, and if he didn't, he'd invent one!

He was also the kind who could drive a car – even an unfamiliar, hired model – with quiet competence and impressive speed. His hands went unerringly to all the right switches. The dashboard light illumined the panel, and also lit up a hawk-nosed, craggy profile. The engine whirred to life, and headlights swept the road ahead as he turned the car expertly, and took them back towards the town.

Nonie lay back against the lumpy upholstery, seething. A hysterical female, he'd called her!

Finally she broke the silence resentfully.

'I hope you don't think I *meant* it when I said I'd whip Pru? I've never so much as laid a finger on her, quite honestly. It was just a – a – an empty threat.'

'Was it?' – sceptically.

'Well, of course it was!' she replied indignantly. 'You don't really think—?'

The wide shoulders shrugged, maddeningly.

'Leave it, little one. What does it matter what I think?'

He had a point there, certainly. Nonie, rebuffed, yet still strangely dissatisfied, relapsed into a huffy silence.

She could not keep it up for long.

'What have you done with your horse?' she asked now, unable to contain her curiosity.

'I've bushed him.'

'Bushed him?'

'Turned him loose.'

'Won't he wander away?'

'He won't go far. He's lame – cast a shoe. That's why I was leading him in the first place.'

'Oh, I see.' A pause. 'Had you led him far?'

His lips twitched.

'Far enough, Miss Gotthart, but I'm hardly decrepit yet, fortunately. If I hadn't been taking a short cut home on foot, I wouldn't have seen you standing there in the darkening like a lost Sioux princess.'

'A – *what*?'

'Winona, the Indian first-born daughter.' He was laughing at her. 'Didn't you know that's what it means?'

'It's spelt with an "e".'

'Same thing, "i" or "e". It's not a usual name.'

'My friends call me Nonie.' She couldn't resist that one,

31

spoken with precisely the same inflection on the word 'friends' as he had given it himself.

He ignored the thrust, except perhaps for the faintest tightening of the level mouth.

'That fairness isn't Sioux. It's almost teutonic – Gotthart. Are you German?'

'Our father was.'

Our father. Our father, which art in Heaven. No, that was Father, capital F. *Our* father was German, small 'f'. And *my* father was Irish. And *my* father's in Heaven, too. Poor Dermot. Poor dreamer.

And poor first-born daughter. No, not first-born, but *only* born. Only daughter, because poor Dermot hadn't waited in this world long enough to have another child. Poor Dermot had – had—

No, maybe he hadn't, after all. It *could* have been an accident, even Bundy had admitted that much. It *could* have been.

Oh, lord, what a mess life could be! Such a muddle—

'Please! Could you stop the car?' she managed to gasp.

'What?' The man glanced her way swiftly.

'I'm going to be sick,' Nonie said urgently.

'Nonie always gets sick if she's a passenger,' explained Pru helpfully, from the back seat. 'Nonie gets sick even in the front. Nonie always says it's different if she's dr—'

But the man didn't wait to hear. He had already brought the car to a skidding halt, leaned across and flung open Nonie's door, and Nonie staggered quietly out into the night and away amongst the trees. There she knelt at the bole of a mottled eucalypt, leaned dizzily against its sustaining trunk. She leaned there until someone pulled her away firmly, and held her head, quite expertly.

She felt the man's hand clamped calmly across her brow and when the spasm had passed, he pressed a handkerchief into her palm. She accepted it wordlessly, allowed herself to be drawn back against his chest, help-less, humiliated beyond belief.

'I'm terribly sorry.'

'No, stay there a minute yet. You'll be better soon.' His hand was still there, keeping her head against his shirt. Presently he turned her around to face him and wiped the dew from her forehead, watching her speculatively.

'Better now?'

She nodded. 'I'm terribly sorry,' she muttered again. Her voice trembled with the sheer shame of it.

'No, it's I who am sorry.' He helped her to her feet with grave, unembarrassed courtesy. It seemed that Jacey Lomax could be quite kind when he chose. Kind, pro-vided that *you* were weaker than *he* was, she decided shrewdly – and she undoubtedly was, right now! She was oddly reluctant to abandon the support of his arm around her. Nonie almost groaned aloud. The indignity of it – that she couldn't stand properly without his help, that he had been there to see her like this!

'All right?' His eyes were crinkling in the moonlight, almost as if he had guessed her thoughts.

'Yes, thank you.' She would have pulled away, but he kept an iron hold on her arm right back to the car.

There he paused, asked solemnly,

'Would you prefer to drive?'

'No, I'll be all right. I think I'm too tired to drive. You were right – I'd have made a hash of it.'

A grin hovered. 'Is that an olive-branch, by any chance? A pipe of peace from the Sioux maiden?' She could see his teeth gleaming in the swarthy tan of his face, as the grin spread and his lips parted. 'I think I prefer the Teutonic tigress to the submissive Sioux, after all,' Jacey Lomax taunted lazily, as he saw her seated once more.

'So you *did* think it funny!' she flashed, anger bringing an immediate stain to her pale cheeks. 'I knew you did! I just knew you were laughing, all the time!'

'Let's just say that I didn't expect to see you on your knees quite so soon after that bristling display of independence back there,' he admitted satirically.

'I think you're hateful!' Her words were muffled, choked with rage.

'Yes, I know. You thought it from the word go.'

How that soothing tone could irritate! He probably knew that, too.

'I hope I never set eyes on you again, *ever*!' she stormed furiously, her blue gaze flashing darkly. And then she remembered to whom it was that she was speaking, after all. To none other than Jacey Lomax. The owner of the house that she wanted so very, very badly. 'I mean – what I mean—'

'You're thinking of the house,' he supplied, uncannily. 'Well, don't worry, Miss Gotthart. If it becomes available, you may deal direct with my estate office. I know how you feel. You're sore as hell at being sick in front of a man, but believe, me, you needn't be. I've a pack of nephews and nieces, and it's not the first time I've helped out. You must have seen for yourself I'm a dab hand at it.'

Monstrous creature! she thought wearily, leaning back and shutting her eyes. First he'd called her a hysterical female, and now he was as good as telling her that she was just another child.

When they reached the hotel, it was to discover that Pru was sound asleep. In her skimpy cotton print frock, she was lying full length along the back seat, one hand on her cheek, the other dangling over the edge of the bench.

'I'll take her. Where's your room?'

Already Jacey Lomax had stooped and gathered the child carefully into his arms. Without speaking further, he followed Nonie up the stairs and into the bedroom, where he laid Pru gently on the bed without waking her up. He'd probably done that hundreds of times too, with those nephews and nieces of whom he spoke.

At the door he turned. 'Good night, Miss Gotthart,' he said levelly.

'What about the car? How will you get back to Tuck-arimba?'

'I'll take it back now. One of my men can bring it back in, in the morning. I'll square the garage.'

'Thank you all the same, but *I* shall pay the garage,' she corrected him crisply. 'I hired the car, after all. Besides, I prefer not to feel in your debt in even the smallest way.'

'Not even the smallest?' There was a glint in his eye that told her he was recalling, as she was, the indisputable comfort of his hold in her recent distress, the steadying contact of that rough masculine palm against her perspiring brow. The right touch, at the right time!

'You've done quite enough,' she told him stiltedly, unable to subdue a rosy blush. 'Good-bye.'

The man inclined his head, twirled the wide-brimmed hat in his brown fingers. 'Good night.' And he was gone.

'Mr. Lomax?' Nonie opened the door and dashed after the long, retreating figure.

'Well?'

'Mr. Lomax, what was your asking price for the old homestead – *if* you sell, I mean?'

'A pause.

'Twelve thousand dollars.'

'Twelve *thousand*?' Her breath caught on the words.

The Lomax man was watching her. In the light of the illumined hall his eyes were a clear, hard grey, cool as a mountain waterfall. They flickered, narrowed.

'Does that seem a lot to you?' he asked. The question came with a sort of quiet, deliberate care.

'No. No, of course not.' She looked away. 'It's worth all of that, I'm sure.'

'It's a gift at the price. There are the orchards and river land included. That puts a mere token value on the house and outbuildings. I'm not out to make a profit on it. Rather let's say that, when and if the time comes, I prefer to dispose of it to the right person, who will of necessity be my close neighbour.'

'Yes, I see your point,' she conceded awkwardly. 'Well, thank you for telling me, anyway.'

She didn't look back, but Nonie had a feeling that he was still standing at the end of the hall when she reached her room again and shut the door behind her.

Next morning, over breakfast, she pondered her problems. Twelve thousand dollars was an awful lot of money. She had barely a quarter of that amount. It was enough to raise a loan, maybe, but with interest to pay too, it was imperative that she keep what capital she had intact. Not only intact – she'd need to try to *add* to it somehow. That meant a job, and moving out of here to cheaper lodgings immediately.

Nonie sighed. She had a feeling that she had been through all this before. It was tough on Pru, too, that her promised freedom would have to be postponed. She told the child as gently as she could.

'But at least we'll be in this pretty town, Pru, and we can get to know the people while we're waiting. You'll be able to start school on Monday. It's right next to the park. I'll take you down and show you, and then you can play on the swings and roundabout for a while, and I'll make fresh arrangements for us.'

'O.K., Nonie.'

Oh, to be eight years old, and have the decisions and responsibilities taken out of one's hands. Pru had taken the news with philosophical cheerfulness, knowing that Nonie would soon come up with some other alternative. She always did!

'Can I go swimming?'

'Better not, just for this morning. I may be quite a while. Stick to the swings and things just for today, poppet.'

'O.K., Nonie.'

Afterwards, Nonie consulted the proprietor of the hotel. He was middle-aged, quite understanding, even helpful in an avuncular sort of way. He eyed her doubtfully.

'A job? The only easy job to come by is domestic work, nobody wants that these days. The little girl could be a problem there, unless it was in a hotel or something. No, we've nothing at all here in the way of vacancies, miss, as you can see. Your best bet would be the Pink Pelican. They're always short-staffed because nobody ever stays for long,' he informed her depressingly.

'Would they take Pru as well?'

'They'd take Pru, and your granny too, if you were willing to sign on. You'd better go down and ask. The big ugly pink place, at the far end of the street going out of town. You'd have passed it coming from the strip. You can't miss it.'

Well, he was right about that, thought Nonie soberly, as she walked across the concrete courtyard to the door of the Pink Pelican. It wasn't the sort of place one could overlook. In fact, it was almost incredible in its ugliness and dinginess. The walls were of that nasty, unsubtle shade often referred to as 'lolly', and the window frames were brown, peeling in places to show that before that they had been cream, and by the look of the odd deeper chip, even green at one time. The pelican that dangled from his rusty hinges over the portico wasn't pink at all, and probably never had been. He was a dirty grey colour, with an orange beak with a broken tip, and one of his legs was missing. Or maybe he had only ever had one leg, standing on it in contemplation in the way a heron does.

37

Inside the Pink Pelican, Nonie's request to join the staff was met with even more enthusiasm than predictions had led her to expect. They were very short-handed, they explained, and no, they didn't mind the youngster, so long as she kept out of the public premises and away from the front of the building. There was a place at the back where she could play around while Nonie herself was occupied, and if Nonie didn't mind long hours, she could earn some overtime pay as well. The money was good, if people were willing to work for it.

Nonie trudged back to the park to report to Pru on her success. Then they went back to have lunch, and in the afternoon they moved their things down to the Pink Pelican. On the way Nonie called at the car-hire garage, and paid her account. The car had been returned that morning by one of Mr. Lomax's station hands, just as he had promised.

The room which Nonie was to share with Pru was in an annexe at the back of the place. The annexe was hardly more than a long weatherboard hut, whose single width was taken up by one identical room after another, with access from a corridor running down the side. This long shed had obviously been added on as staff quarters, but at the moment all of the rooms were empty except for their own and one other, occupied by a plump, henna-haired woman in her forties, who told Nonie that she was the 'still-room maid'. Nonie was to discover, in the weeks that followed, that the 'still-room maid' had a roving commission, rushing from place to place wherever she might be most urgently wanted, just as Nonie herself had to do, because of the inadequacy of the help on hand.

That first night she spent altering the hems of the black uniforms with which they had provided her, and running-in the sides of the garments to give them a better fit. She turned the procedure into a fun thing for Pru's benefit, folding and tilting the white caps at the different angles, and there was much giggling between them as they pirouetted in front of the mirror, posturing and making faces at each other. But inside herself, Nonie could not quell her doubts and misgivings. She knew this was not the sort of place she would have chosen to take Pru, yet it seemed the best that offered at the moment. Her misgivings extended further, to her own abilities, her lack of experience. What if she proved to be inefficient, and they dismissed her?

She need not, as it turned out, have worried on that score. Far from dismissing her, they worked her to the bone, but as they had promised, they paid her well for doing so. She was kept at it till late at night, and therefore she hardly saw Pru after school, but was able to arrange her hours so that they could at least breakfast together before she saw the little girl off in the morning.

In the first few weeks, the early rising and late nights, the heavy physical activity, took their toll of Nonie. Her muscles ached, her limbs felt leaden, and her hands became red and raw, although she creamed them diligently each evening before she flopped thankfully into bed. If she had been thin before, she was almost ethereal now.

And then, after a month or so, she seemed to get her second wind. Not only was she more accustomed to the constancy of her varied chores, but there was also the satisfaction of finding that Pru, too, had reached the same stage with her schooling. She seemed to be enjoying her lessons, by all accounts, and made proper friends with whom she stayed playing in the park until tea-time. Once Nonie had assured herself that there were responsible attendants at the baths, she gave her consent to swimming sessions as well. Pru would come in from these with a ravenous appetite, and the plain, reasonably wholesome food at evening tea would disappear in a flash. All the time, the pay packets mounted regularly, and any time when Nonie was particularly weary, or inclined to be a little depressed, she would buck herself up by remembering her goal – the dear old homestead at Tuckarimba, with its little orchard and the extra acres for the market garden that she hoped some day to make hers.

This evening she had had an especially trying day, and was now in the room behind the bar, sluicing glasses and slinging them back through the hatch to the counter. It was a Friday night, and the 'still-room maid' had chosen to take her half-day, rather than count it as extra hours, which was what she had always done before. Nonie had been sent to fill in for her, and so far things hadn't gone too badly.

The noise was deafening. It came in great gusts of sound every time the still-room door swung back on its hinges. The place was packed. Every time Nonie went through to scoop up an armful of used glasses, she marvelled at the thickness of the atmosphere, the wafting clouds of smoke, the sticky smell of heavy beer.

And they called this fun!

She had just returned a tray of clean glasses through the hatch, and was in the act of gathering up some more empty ones at the end of the counter when the scuffling broke out in the corner where she was. Scuffling, at *first*. But with the most alarming rapidity it developed into what could only be described as a good-going fight.

Nonie cowered against the wall. Nobody seemed to be taking any notice of her at all, which was of some comfort, as she was effectively hedged in all of a sudden. The men about her were by now too busy hurling lewd epithets at each other, and battering each other with clenched fists that seemed to her widening eyes as big as outsized hams. She had never seen anything like it in her life! She could only stand there, ducking instinctively as she saw the blows landing, gasped with horror as blood commenced to spurt and bruised eyes to close.

'Stop! *Stop* it, I say!'

But of course they ignored her pleas. To be truthful, Nonie doubted if they even heard them.

Her horror increased. She had to get out of here. She *must* get out! Somehow she stiffened her faltering limbs, and sidled along the wall towards the door.

'Not going, gorgeous?'

He was young, quite good-looking in a way, with his white shirt and tie, his best town garb. He was also very drunk. He pulled himself away from the table where one of his adversaries had just flung him, leering amiably around, as if enjoying the mêlée. As Nonie dashed past he made a grab at her.

'Hey there, c'mon! The party's only starting!'

She snatched herself away, felt the bib of her neat white apron torn from its pin. As the young man's fingers caught her cap that, too, came off and fell to the floor, somewhere in amongst the pounding feet.

'Let me *go*!'

She groped amongst the flailing legs, retrieved the crumpled remains of her frilly white headgear, and at last managed to escape, into the air outside.

Nonie had never been so relieved in all her life. For a moment she simply leaned against the wall, panting to recover her breath. Then she held her cap between her teeth as she attempted to pin up her tumbling, fair mane into the neat coil upon which the little white bonnet had been perched. Her fingers were trembling to such an extent that the task was well-nigh impossible.

'Drat it!' she muttered in frustration, then her hands paused in their task as a man came with long strides over the concrete towards the entrance near where she stood. A tall man, he was. A man in pale, neatly-creased drill trousers, and polished boots, and a crisp white shirt with a cravat knotted casually at the throat. A man with thick black hair and scowling brows, and eyes that were a piercing grey in the mellow light from the doorway.

'Good grief! *You!*' The eyes had fastened themselves on her huddled form, in the semi-dark a little way along the wall.

'What are *you* doing here?' Jacey Lomax sounded surprised, and somehow angry.

'Oh, Mr. Lomax – *please*—' She pushed herself away from the wall, relief washing over her at the sight of someone she knew. Someone *responsible*. 'Please, Mr. Lomax, go in and stop them,' she gasped. 'They'll listen to you! They – they're killing each other in there. Do hurry! They'll *listen* to you, you see.' Her eyes were wild, her voice taut high with strain.

Nonie's fingers returned, distractedly, to her hair. Oh, this wretched hair! It had tumbled down all over again, spilling over her shoulders, almost to her waist. The comb which had secured it fell too. She stooped to retrieve it, then followed the direction of the man's gaze. Ineffectually she tried to cover the rent in the front of her dress, where the pin had caught and torn it.

'Here, let me.' Jacey Lomax took the pin from her fumbling fingers and turned her towards the light. His face was completely without expression as he brought the pieces of black material together, covered them with the flap of frilled white cotton that was her apron-bib, and slid the pin through, fastening it deftly. He took not the slightest notice of the thuds, curses, bumps and shouting that still emanated from the room beyond them.

'Why are you here?' he said again. 'Miss Gotthart, will you leave that blasted thing for the moment and *answer* me!' he barked suddenly, taking the squashed cap from her and ramming it into his pocket.

'I work here. But what about you?'

'I've come for my men. They're in there.' A careless jerk of the dark head towards the door.

In there? His men? And he sounded as though he

couldn't care less!

'They're not men, they're monsters. Jungle beasts, or worse. If they're yours, I advise you to get them out as speedily as possible,' she urged him coldly, 'before they succeed in bashing each other to a pulp.'

He shrugged. 'It wouldn't be the first time.'

'*And* they're wrecking the place – the furniture – some of the tables are matchwood already, and – and chairs – glasses—' Nonie gestured impressively, yet he remained *un*impressed.

'Not the first time, either.' The man seemed to find her remarks amusing. 'The usual procedure,' he went on to inform her, 'after *this* sort of spree, is, I pay the pub, and the men pay me. In other words, they don't mind paying for their fun.'

'Fun! You call that fun?'

'*I* don't, but *they* do.' A smile lurked somewhere in the depths of the level grey eyes that were still looking down at her. 'Haven't you heard how the song goes?

"When we go to spree in town

We live like pigs in clover?" '

'No, I haven't' – her voice was tart – 'but the words are apt, that much strikes me quite forcibly!' She shuddered, in spite of herself, and then found to her dismay that somehow she couldn't stop. Even her teeth were chattering, although it was a warm night.

'Did they hurt you?' he asked instantly, and Nonie guessed by the swift concern in his voice that she must look as white and witless as she felt.

'No, not me, but each other.' Her voice trembled. 'They'll murder each other, I tell you.'

'The hell they will. They never quite manage to go as far as that, although I reckon there'll be a few jokers in there feeling pretty sorry for themselves in the morning. You should know better than to intervene.'

'I – wasn't – intervening.' She pushed her hair back

indignantly, looked up at him with candid, hollow eyes that still felt glazed with fright. 'I was trying to get away, and I nearly did, I was – qu-quite n-near the d-door when one of them grabbed me. I don't think he even knew wh-what he was d-doing—'

'Possibly not.' He pressed his lips together. 'Come with me.'

Jacey Lomax took her arm and led her around the side of the building, towards the portico where the dirty grey pelican danced sadly on his one leg from the iron hinges. She had no option but to go where he was taking her, because his grasp was firm and curiously unrelenting.

When they reached the porch, she resisted.

'I'm not supposed to go in the front. I don't think you understand.'

'At the moment you are my guest,' he told her crushingly.

Inside, he pushed her down into a chair in the lounge and jabbed at the bell on the wall.

'Yes, Mr. Lomax?' The proprietor's eyes widened as they took in the identity of Mr. Lomax's companion.

'Bring me a beer, please, will you, and a brandy for the lady. And a pot of tea for two.' Jacey Lomax's snapping eyes were forbidding questions.

'Yes, Mr. Lomax.'

'I reckon things are getting a bit wild through there at the back. You'd better send Fred and Stanley to cool them down. I'll settle with you later, as usual.'

'Most certainly, Mr. Lomax.'

'Are all those men yours?' asked Nonie weakly, when the proprietor had gone away.

'Only four. The others are from surrounding stations, and some from the town itself. Thanks, Barney. Just put them there.'

Jacey Lomax waited while the other man placed the drinks and tea on the table between them, and when he had gone away again passed her a small glass with the brandy in it.

'Skol!' He held up his own tall tankard of frothing beer.

'Er – Skol,' she replied gallantly, matching his gesture with hers. She loathed spirits, but tonight she had a feeling that she needed this!

Nonie sipped in silence, and then, because the taste was so repellent, took the last part of her drink at a gulp, and lay back, closing her eyes as the fiery stuff coursed through her bracingly. She heard the chink of crockery as he poured the tea, and then a subdued rustling brought her eyes open again.

Jacey Lomax was rolling himself a cigarette, tilting the rubbed tobacco carefully from his brown palm on to a wafer of paper.

'You don't object?'

She shook her head. 'Please do.'

'Take your tea now.' His lighter flared, and he leaned back, drawing deeply on the neat cylinder he had just fashioned. When he had made sure it was alight satisfactorily, he looked up. 'Feeling steadier?'

'Yes, thank you.'

'Then maybe you'd care to answer that question I asked you several times out there, and which you thought you'd successfully dispatched.'

'I don't understand.'

'I think you do. Why *here*?' He leaned forward, his eyes hard.

'Why what here?'

'Why work here?' He was being heavily patient, his voice level.

Nonie put down her cup and shrugged, a little flippantly.

'Why not? Some people have to work for a living, Mr. Lomax.'

45

'Granted.' He watched her through a curl of smoke. 'Now try again.'

She licked her lips. The man's composure was extraordinarily unnerving.

'The – the pay's good,' she said defensively. 'And they don't mind having Pru along with me. Her board and lodging are thrown in. That's quite a big consideration.'

Jacey Lomax smoked in silence for a while. It seemed to be a very thoughtful silence indeed. Then—

'Haven't you and the kid really got a home to go to?'

'We're waiting to get into it,' she told him pointedly, and was rewarded to see a tinge of colour darkening his tan. There was something about this domineering creature that made her itch to needle him, and Nonie was inordinately pleased with herself at having succeeded.

'Haven't you a home to go *back* to? You know perfectly well what I mean! Where did you come from? Sydney? They told me you got off the Sydney plane.'

So he'd been making inquiries, had he? Well, in a way that was natural, to want to know where a potential buyer for your house had come from, especially when the old and new homesteads happened to be so close to one another. She had better be reasonable over this, although she felt resentful of his interference, tempted to tell him to mind his own business.

'Yes, Sydney.'

'Well then?'

'We only had rooms there, the same as we have here. There was no point in returning. In any case, travelling can be expensive, and I want to be easily accessible to your – er – estate office.'

'What sort of work did you do in Sydney? Not this?'

'Not exactly this.'

'What?'

'Oh, this and that.' She shrugged a little helplessly. 'It's difficult to explain. I'd done a course in design and sign-writing, but the commercial prospects are overrated. I mean, once you've got a sign, you don't think about changing it for years. Somehow everyone seemed to have signs, after a while.'

'What else?'

'Oh, all sorts of things. Picture-framing. There was an art gallery that used to put stuff my way. But I don't see an art gallery in Tucka, and everyone has signs already, haven't they?'

'Your parents?'

'They're dead.' Her tone didn't invite sympathy. She got up, smoothed her apron down over the drab black crêpe of her dress. 'Thanks for the tea, and the drink, Mr. Lomax. You probably saved my life, and certainly my honour!' She laughed a little huskily, turned towards the hall, and remarked brightly, 'Well, I'd better return to the nether regions, or I might be feeling as sorry for myself in the morning as those men of yours, if for different reasons! Chambermaids aren't encouraged to loll around in the front lounge drinking brandy with the patrons!'

She hadn't gone two steps when he caught her up. It had only taken one of his long strides to do it. Another brought him in front of her, right in her path. Now she felt both her wrists grasped firmly, halting her in her tracks.

'You stubborn little fool!' Jacey Lomax's voice had gone deep and rough. His eyes held the grey steeliness of controlled anger. 'You can't go on with this business, and you know it. Hell, you'll fade away, crack up. You're white as paper, thin as a wraith, and your nerves are jangling like fire-buckets underneath all that calm. In fact, you're as taut as a fiddle-string, and you look like nothing on earth, if you want the truth.'

'Well, *thanks*,' she drawled sarcastically, and there was

a flash of pure rebellion in her own eyes as she tried to draw away.

His mouth levelled. A muscle flicked at the side of his cheek.

'You know well enough what I'm trying to tell you. You must see what you're doing to yourself? Why, if I hadn't seen that pale hair dangling around your face out there in the half-light, I mightn't have recognized you at all.'

'Then perhaps it's a pity you did,' she retorted coldly – and that made him release her wrists instantly.

'If that's how you feel about it, then I, too, regret it.' The man's eyes were as cool as his tone. 'I'll say good night, Miss Gotthart.'

There was just the hint of a formal bow, and then he went back to the table, stubbed his cigarette butt into the cheap tin ash-tray with the beer advertisement running round the sides.

'Mr. Lomax?' Nonie had remembered something. 'Could I have my cap, please?'

He took it from his pocket without a word.

'Thanks.' To her dismay Nonie's voice was wobbling, and tears had unaccountably filled her eyes. She hated making enemies, and it seemed that tonight she certainly had. 'I'm sorry if I seem ungrateful,' she told him in a tight voice. 'I know you meant it kindly.'

He was searching her face. His own features were set in granite lines. The sheer inscrutability of the man made Nonie dither.

'I – I don't expect you to understand,' she said a little desperately, looking away, 'but I simply can't afford for people to be *kind*. It's a quality just as easily withdrawn as it is bestowed, and if it's *there*, one is tempted to lean on it. It's a risk I just can't take. Please say you understand? Just a little bit?'

Her eyes came up to his, misty with pleading. His were

unreadable. Unmoved.

'I'm not as slow as you appear to think,' said Jacey Lomax slowly. 'I had got the message already.'

There was a quiet irony in his voice that told Nonie he hadn't really got it at all. Her explanation had been completely misunderstood.

The knowledge of it filled her with an unfamiliar, fatalistic despair as she walked away to resume her duties. She had emerged from this encounter strangely bruised, and there was a curious little pain that lingered yet, somewhere inside her chest.

CHAPTER THREE

'Seems like you ain't ter relieve me in drinking hours ever again, after last night's escapade,' said Doris of the henna hair next morning. 'So that's the last of me Friday nights out till they can get someone else ter do it instead.'

'Who said so?' Nonie was indignant. 'It wasn't *my* fault they all started fighting like a bunch of grizzlies, was it?'

'Jacey Lomax said so. Gave it ter Barney straight.'

'And what business is it of his, may I ask?' Nonie found that she was really nettled. The Lomax man still seemed to have that particular effect upon her, and a few additional ones as well that were far harder to define!

'I reckon Jacey don't like his men lookin' like a case of squashed plums when 'e's wantin' them ter do a muster for 'im next morning,' explained Doris nasally. 'You gotter be *firm* with 'em, ducks, these blokes. You gotter be *tough*, see. It's the only language that lot recognize.' She sighed. 'Maybe it takes an older woman ter keep 'em in order, more experienced than what you are.'

'It's not *my* place to discipline Jacey Lomax's men, or any other,' Nonie returned tartly.

'Funny, that's just exactly what Jacey was sayin' ter Barney when I come in last night, them words exactly. Yer didn't get together on it by any chance, did yer?' Doris's tone was dry.

'You know I didn't, Dorrie. I – I can't stand the man. He's nothing but an interfering autocrat.'

'Big words, fer a big fella.' Doris giggled. 'You better not let the rest of the town hear you talkin' about Jacey like that. He's the kingpin around 'ere, yer know, and 'e's real popular, too. Does a lot of decent things fer people on the Q.T., does Jacey. And yer gotter admit 'e looks – well – wow! – real class.' She shrugged her plump shoulders comically. 'I wish 'e'd take *me* ter the front lounge fer a bit of a booze-up now and then. I could really go **fer** them big, lazy grey eyes 'n lovely white teeth, and if 'e put 'is arm around *me* and led *me* to a chair like Barney said 'e did with you – cripes! I'd pass out on the blinkin' spot.'

'And where would that get you?' asked Nonie practically.

'Well, I don't *know* about *where—*' Doris's voice trailed away dreamily. Her pouchy eyes were narrowed in what was obviously some sort of pleasant speculation.

'Oh, come on, Dorrie. I've got work to do, even if you haven't.'

Nonie flounced away impatiently. She had heard and seen enough of Jacey Lomax to last her a lifetime, and she did wish that everyone around here would let the subject drop.

After that, she was not asked to perform that particular duty again, which meant that Barney must be in as much awe of the Lomax man as the rest of the population. The days wore on, and the incident receded in Nonie's own mind, and apparently in everyone else's too, since it was not referred to again. As it turned out, she was given other things to think about anyway – surprising things. *Worrying* things.

She gazed at the headmaster in horror.

'You mean, Pru hasn't been going to school each day, as I thought? All this time, when I've been congratulating myself upon how well she has settled down, she has in fact been playing hookey?'

'So Miss Wilson in Primary Two tells me.'

'For – for how long? I mean, how many times has she done it?' asked Nonie faintly, trying to grasp the import of the information she had just received.

'Too often,' responded the headmaster grimly. 'We don't know the specific number of instances, because at first the teacher thought she'd been unwell. Then, when she demanded a note from you, as her guardian, none was forthcoming. I admit that she's not alone in the crime, but you understand that we have to nip it in the bud, otherwise the idea of skipping lessons will soon spread. We had no choice but to inform you, Miss Gotthart, and seek your co-operation in the matter.'

'Yes, of course, I understand that.' Nonie sat down weakly. 'I can't think – I mean, why should she begin to do a thing like that? She never has before.'

'Possibly it's as Mr. Lomax says – a lack of stability in her background.'

'Her background?'

'Her home life. In fact, in a nutshell, a *lack* of home life.'

'Mr. Lomax! How does he come into it?' Nonie's eyes were resentful. She could feel them growing round, incredulous, as spots of uncomfortable colour stained her cheeks at the mere mention of that man's name.

'He's the convenor of the Education Committee. It came up at the monthly meeting.'

'Why wasn't I told before it reached that stage? Surely, if it's been going on for a while, I should have been the first to know?'

To think that Jacey Lomax knew things about her little sister that she didn't even know herself! It was an impossible situation!

'Each case is treated individually. In this particular instance, it was regarded as preferable to allow the child's teacher to try to deal with the matter first. Had she been successful, you would not have been worried with it at all.'

'And she hasn't been successful? I see.' Nonie swallowed miserably. 'Well, I shall speak to Pru in no uncertain terms, you may be sure. It does seem as if now is the time to play the heavy parent.'

She attempted a smile, but somehow it didn't quite come off. Pru playing truant! It had never happened before, and she hadn't the foggiest idea as to how she was going to tackle it.

'That's just it, Miss Gotthart.' The schoolmaster looked grave. He wasn't even trying to answer her tentative smile. 'As Mr. Lomax said, you *aren't* a parent. Therein probably lies the root of the problem.'

'It will be no problem,' Nonie asserted, suddenly cool and formal and very firm indeed. 'You may safely leave it to me. I've managed perfectly well as a substitute parent up to this moment, and Mr. Lomax oversteps himself in presuming to comment on that angle. He knows extraordinarily little about our case, so little that I regard it as presumption on his part to even pass an opinion!'

The other shrugged, unwilling to commit himself. 'You'll see about it, then?' The headmaster raised his hat, and Nonie, still seething, yet managed to see him politely to the door.

To her dismay, Pru's own reactions confirmed all too clearly that there was some foundation, at least, in Jacey Lomax's analysis of the situation. Nonie felt first surprise, then dismay, and finally a sort of winded helplessness.

'But, Pru, why? Why?'

'I didn't think you'd mind, Nonie.'

'Not mind? Darling, of course I mind. I mind very much indeed. Whatever could have given you such an idea?'

The little girl shuffled her feet uncomfortably.

'Well, I mean, you're never around, Nonie. You're never *there* any more, are you? You don't worry about what I'm doing when I muck around by myself at the back of this stinky old building, so I didn't think you'd care about the daytime, either.'

'Well, I *do* care! And in *school hours* – Oh, Pru, how could you be so deceitful? And here was I, thinking how well you were getting on with your lessons.'

'I wasn't, though,' mumbled Pru unhappily. 'It's all different, what we have out here. I couldn't get my arithmetic to add up, and I'd never done geography, I can't begin to understand it. I wanted to ask you, sometimes, but you weren't around. You always seemed to be so busy doing something else. And I meant to tell you, too, the first time we played up and didn't go to school, but you were so busy then too, and I – well, I just didn't, that's all. I'd have probably said it to you, like I used to when you were doing the picture-frames in the corner or something, or when you were typing I could have, or weeding the path. We used to tell each other everything, didn't we, only here there isn't much of a chance – not that I don't like it *much* better here,' she hastened to add, her eyes fastened in some anxiety on her sister's anguished face.

'No, Pru, I – I can see how it happened. It was as much my fault as yours, darling. But that doesn't mean it can happen again. It mustn't, *ever*, do you understand? Promise me on your honour, Pru.'

'Cross my heart and spit my death.'

'And—' Nonie hesitated – 'this won't be for much longer, Pru, living this way. It's just a – a very temporary arrangement. I know it's not very satisfactory for either of us, but it was the best I could do at the time. I'll try for something different, better, but I don't suppose I'll have much luck.' She stifled a sigh. 'Schooling is important, though, and from now on I'm going to make myself available for a while each afternoon when you come back, and we'll go over everything you did that day in lessons. That way I'll know whether you really *have* been to school or not.'

She made herself sound severe, but inside she could only feel a mute self-reproach.

The unhappy, 'trapped' feeling persisted. Even though she kept her word and met Pru each afternoon for as long as she could possibly spare, and made up the time she had taken with extra work after the child was in bed, Nonie found that she was still worrying, sleeping badly.

When Jacey Lomax appeared out of nowhere a couple of weeks later, he, too, seemed as aware as she was herself of the way in which her skin was drawn so tightly over her high cheekbones, and of the new hollows that made smudgy shadows beneath her dark-lashed blue eyes.

'Are you well?'

Jacey asked the question abruptly, spinning his broad-brimmed hat on to the small round tea-table in the lounge to which he had summoned her, and turning to where she waited politely in the doorway.

'Perfectly, thanks.'

'Hmm.' He gave her an assessing look, but made no further comment as he saw her seated, then hitched the legs of his khaki moleskin trousers and took a chair himself, stretching out his long limbs in their polished elastic-sided boots.

He came straight to the point.

'I've come to offer you a job.'

'But I already have one.' She looked at him in some surprise.

He made a dismissive gesture. 'What I have in mind could be more suitable.' His mouth levelled as he observed her expression. 'It's not working for *me*,' he emphasized bitingly, 'so keep an open mind for a few minutes if you *possibly* can, will you, Miss Gotthart?'

'Who is it for, then?' she asked cautiously.

'For my brother, actually.' A pause. 'Out at Tuckarimba.'

'Tuckarimba?'

'At the old place.'

'You mean at the old homestead?' Her eyes widened as he nodded half impatiently.

'Raynor is there now, recovering, we hope, from a pole accident. Unfortunately there's a doubt as to how complete that recovery will ever become, which is why I postponed the disposal of the house in the meantime. He's accustomed to country life and was fretting badly in the hospital, so it seemed a good idea to get him up here, near enough to me to keep an eye on his progress, but where he could at the same time be reasonably independent.'

And how independent could you be, Nonie was asking herself somewhat acidly, if Jacey Lomax himself had decided to keep an eye on you? Poor brother!

Aloud she asked,

'What is the matter with your brother exactly, Mr. Lomax? I'm afraid I have no nursing qualifications whatsoever.'

She watched him searching his pockets, slapping them one after the other in his hunt for his tobacco and papers. When he found where they were he took them out and began to roll himself a cigarette with slow preoccupation.

'Ray's past that stage now, more or less,' he told her, rubbing the tobacco between his palms half absently. 'What he's needing now is a different approach altogether.' He gave her a direct look. 'You see, Miss Gotthart, Raynor can't walk. He's in a wheel-chair, and that's where he'll very likely remain for the rest of his days unless he can in some way be persuaded out of it.' He sounded grim.

'I see.'

'No, you don't, and neither do the rest of us. The doctors confirm that there's now no apparent medical reason why he shouldn't be able to walk again, but the fact is that he can't, and won't even attempt it. There was a certain amount of spinal damage at the time of his fall, but not so serious that it should have resulted in permanent disability. They're convinced that Ray could walk if he'd only try it, but for some reason he won't even put himself to the test.'

Nonie wasn't looking at Jacey Lomax now, because she didn't want him to be aware of the compassion she was feeling for the young man whose life had been so cruelly altered by what must have been a terrible misfortune. Compassion was a weakness, and Nonie knew that if Jacey Lomax spotted it, he'd ferret it out and play on it, because that was probably what it suited him to do. She also knew that she wasn't up to this kind of thing at all – which was why she looked, not at him, but at his polished boots. Those elastic-sided boots that all the stockmen out here seemed to wear, with a defined heel and a welted sole and a little tab at the back to pull them on and off.

'I couldn't do it, Mr. Lomax. I couldn't do anything for your brother. I can hardly do anything for myself and Pru, let alone anyone else.' She could not hide her bitterness. 'I'd be quite inadequate.'

'You foolish child!' Nonie's gaze shot upwards at the strange harshness of his tone. 'Do you think I'd saddle *you* with *that* sort of responsibility, when—' He broke off, ran a brown hand through his hair in a way that was somehow quite uncharacteristic of Jacey Lomax's usual calm. 'Just credit me with a little sense and judgment, and trust me, will you?' he said indistinctly. 'You haven't heard me out yet.'

'I'm sorry,' she apologized meekly.

'Your role is only a background one, quite simply.'

The way he said it was reassuring enough to make her pay attention once again. Even while she was registering with vague resentment the fact that he had said 'is' and not 'would be', she was also thinking how nice Jacey Lomax's eyes were when they softened like that. They had become kind, and comforting, and their colour was a

57

deep, almost caressing grey that held none of the water-fall coldness.

'I don't intend to put more responsibility your way, but rather less,' he was now continuing matter-of-factly, like an Army general giving a briefing to a particularly dim underling. 'When Raynor had this accident he broke off his engagement – I'd better put you in the picture about that properly. Ilse was very upset about it indeed, but he insisted on releasing her – did the noble thing, in his own eyes if no one else's. Look, isn't there somewhere else where we can talk? You're obviously on edge in here. Why?'

She shrugged apologetically, lifted her white apron and let it drop again rather helplessly.

'I didn't mean to make it obvious. But you're right, of course. I'm not supposed to be here, chatting to – to the – er – clientele. It makes things a bit awkward with Doris and the rest.'

He stood up.

'When are you free?' he asked abruptly. 'I'll come back.'

Nonie hesitated.

'I have an hour and a half each afternoon now, when Pru comes back from school, so that I can be with her to – er –' to hear how she got on, and things,' she added lamely.

'Have you always done that?'

'It's a new arrangement,' she confessed awkwardly, blushing furiously and hoping he'd leave it. 'I make it up later – the time, I mean.'

He did leave it, thank heaven. She couldn't have borne a lecture from a member of the Education Committee at this point, when she was doing everything she possibly could to get Pru on the right lines again!

'We'll discuss it over a walk,' said Jacey Lomax unexpectedly. 'Pru can come with us and play in the park while we discuss it. I'll be back at—' he glanced at the wristwatch strapped to one hairy brown wrist – 'say, four o'clock.'

'Very well.'

'Be ready.'

He was gone.

Now why did he have to spoil it all by adding that brief command at the end? It snapped Nonie out of the pleasant state into which she had been gradually sliding – an almost companionable state! Nonie found that she was in two minds about her walk with Jacey Lomax. One half of her was back to hating the man for his bossy attitude to all and sundry, the other was contemplating the outing with a faintly tingling anticipation that was at once unfamiliar and disturbing.

She put on her navy linen button-through, and brushed out her long fair hair carefully, but something perverse inside her decided against further preparation or the use of make-up. Her pallor was regrettable, certainly, compared with most of the lovely golden-skinned girls she had seen in the streets of this country town. And she could no doubt have improved her reflection with the application of some additional colour. As she gazed in the mirror, she noted with dissatisfaction that the only vestige of colour in her whole face was the natural pinkness of her lips and the dark glow of her eyes, which had gone the same deep navy as the dress itself.

Yes, she could improve things – but for *that* man, never!

Be ready, he had said, and she was.

Nonie had trouble in keeping up with his long strides as they made their way towards the park. To outpace him she'd have had to run as Pru was already running, a little ahead of them, and that would have been even more undignified than panting along beside him like this, giving only the odd half-skip to keep herself level. If she had envisaged a companionable stroll, then already she was doomed to disappointment!

In the park itself, Jacey Lomax looked a little uncomfortable, slightly out of place, as if he seldom if ever went there. Other people must have thought the same thing, because one or two looked openly surprised as they recognized him and said a mumbled ' 'Day, Jacey' in passing.

'We'll sit here, and Pru can go to the swings.' He indicated a wooden seat with a slatted back and iron legs. 'Have you given some thought to what I was saying earlier?'

Trust Jacey Lomax! Always the disconcertingly direct approach!

'I've been busy,' Nonie hedged.

'Hmm. I can't blame you for not wanting to commit yourself until you've heard the whole set-up.' He sighed. 'The present position is a type of mental and emotional deadlock, so far as my brother is concerned. It will impede his hopes of recovery unless some sort of change takes place. Ilse is herself a physiotherapist. She now wants me to dispense with the nurse, since Ray can virtually look after himself now anyway, and Ilse proposes to come up and stay, providing I can find some sort of chaperone-cum-housekeeper.' At the look on Nonie's face his lip curled sardonically. 'Not a chaperone in the accepted sense of the term, Miss Gotthart. These two are mature people, and Ray is still dead set against taking up where he left off with Ilse – through what I consider to be a misguided highmindedness.'

'Perhaps your brother doesn't see it that way.'

'No matter what way he sees it, Ilse's feelings are involved too. She wants this chance, and I'm determined that she shall have it. You will merely be another presence, to defuse the atmosphere, and give the set-up as much normality as possible. She thinks it's better to come primarily in the role of masseuse and professional therapist, and play down the ex-fiancée bit. It was Ray, after all, who insisted on calling the whole thing off. Ilse still hopes he'll come to his senses about their plans for the future. She thinks that with returning health, propinquity and so on, that this can be achieved. Do you follow me?'

'I think so. It sounds worth a try. But—' hesitating – 'I still don't honestly see where I come in.'

'As I said, your role is a background one. Can you cook?'

'I'm not much good, Mr. Lomax. As I once told you, I'm a jack-of-all-trades, but cooking has never featured either prominently or successfully.'

'So long as you don't actually poison them, you'll do.' His lips twitched.

'I don't think you understand,' she retorted worriedly. 'The only cooking I know is what I've taught myself. I can knock up simple dishes, but I can't pretend to be competent.'

'You'll manage all that's required of you,' he told her with certainty. 'It's only a question of filling in on Hattie's week-ends off. She's been there cooking for the nurse, and she'll carry on for as long as I ask her to. You will be primarily a companion for Ilse.'

Nonie turned to him on the bench, doubt clouding the soft darkness of her glance.

'You don't need me there, Mr. Lomax, do you, if we're to be honest? What's the use of pretending? I – I have the feeling that you – that you're *creating* a place for me in your brother's household where there isn't really a place at all.'

'Rubbish!' Jacey Lomax sounded impatient. He looked at her oddly. 'Why would I do a thing like that?'

'Pity? Charity? Disapproval of my present employment?' She shrugged. 'I don't like people feeling sorry for

61

me. I thought I'd made that clear.'

His lips tightened in a forbidding manner. So did the muscles in his jaw. In fact his features congealed into an awesome severity that made Nonie wonder if she should have been quite so outspoken.

'Listen to me, Miss Gotthart. When I am *sorry* for people, they're not left in any two minds about it, I can assure you.' The words were strangely clipped. 'My pity I reserve for Raynor and Ilse, bogged down in this emotional mess they're in. My charity I keep for those who deserve it, which I can't say I reckon you *do*. As for my feelings about your present work, you know darned well what they are, and I haven't attempted to hide them, have I?'

'No, you haven't, and that's why I find myself wondering now – I mean–' Nonie floundered dubiously.

'What does it take to convince you, Miss Gotthart? If you stop thinking about yourself for a second or two, and turn that introspective little mind of yours outwards for just a moment, perhaps you'll acknowledge that your presence and the child's at Old Tuckarimba could serve a genuinely useful purpose. You'll be expected to do your share in the house, I warn you, and for what you do you will be rewarded commensurately, with board and lodging properly deducted. Does that sound like charity? Like pity? I don't think so! You strike me as having a certain amount of common sense and perception, so you'll appreciate that cheerful feminine company for Ilse, and a child's amusing chatter, could be the right background touches for both of them just now. Besides–' he narrowed his eyes in the direction of Pru's bright, cotton-clad form, pirouetting over the grass – 'there's something very relaxing about a child playing around the place, don't you agree? And Ray has always had a sneaking fondness for kids. That about sums it up, Miss Gotthart. Take it or leave it.'

His brusqueness had a strangely astringent impact upon Nonie. Her mind had been racing, her thoughts tumbling over themselves one after the other. Now the process had steadied itself into an analysis of a quite objective sort.

How could she refuse this chance? It could be painful finding herself back in her old home in these particular circumstances, but it would be better than the present set-up – anything would be! And for Pru it would mean a more family-style life than her impersonal existence here at the Pink Pelican. Tuckarimba was a true home, a place where she would have the freedom to run about where she pleased, instead of being confined to the dingy back premises of this public house, except for daily rambles in the park. She and Nonie could be with each other a lot of the time out there. That was what Pru had been missing, her sister's influence. That was why she had been so naughty, playing truant from school. Indeed, Nonie was finding it increasingly difficult to get through to Pru these days. There was a lack of communication that was beginning to cause her constant and gnawing worry.

'I'll take it, thanks,' she heard herself say, with every bit as much brusqueness as his.

'That's settled, then.' Jacey Lomax stood up, swung around as a musical feminine voice called from the path behind him.

'Jay – cey! Jacey, it *is* you! What a peculiar place to find you in, darling!'

The woman's tone was underlined with a quite satirical amusement that brought a grin to Jacey Lomax's swarthy features.

'You, too, Delphine. One could hardly describe the public park as your – er – natural habitat.'

'I'm taking a short cut to the Golf Club, actually.' The young woman's pretty face held a definite question. What are *you* doing, Jacey? she was asking, just as eloquently as though she had spoken the words aloud.

She was a very attractive person indeed, of medium height, with a slender figure and the shapeliest legs that Nonie had ever seen in her whole life. Perhaps the most striking thing about her, apart from those legs, was that beautiful auburn hair that waved away from her high forehead in burnished glory. Instead of the pale cream complexion that so often goes with rich auburn colouring, this girl's skin was a surprise. She was deeply tanned, the dusting of freckles was curiously fetching, and her long green eyes had the composed glitter of a jungle cat's, the same bold challenge too.

It seemed that Jacey Lomax intended to ignore the unspoken question.

'Miss Gotthart, Miss Simpson.' He introduced the two women, continued easily, 'I'll walk a bit of the way with you, Delphine. Excuse me just a moment, I'll be right back.'

He had settled the broad-brimmed hat back on his head. Now he tipped it in a polite gesture to Nonie and strode off over the grass to join the girl who waited there, a small, satisfied smile lurking round the corner of her gay red mouth.

Just like a kitten that's got first to the bowl of cream, thought Nonie in some amusement, watching the tall broad figure and the dainty feminine one as they walked past the fountain in the direction of the building over there amongst the trees, presumably the club-house.

The two were deep in conversation. Nonie wondered idly if they were speaking about her. She supposed that Jacey Lomax would find it necessary to explain his unexpected presence there on a bench in the public park.

When he came back, he gave no indication whatever of the possible nature of his conversation with his woman friend. He was jingling the loose change in his trouser-pocket in a rather absentminded manner, as if perhaps his thoughts were still with his recent companion.

He brought his mind back to Nonie with a slight frown.

'Yes. Well, let's see. Where were we?' The beetling brows scowled a little. 'You have agreed to take the position?'

'Yes.'

'Splendid. Then I'll speak to your present employer, and fix things up. No need for you to be personally involved. I'll handle it for you. I dare say Barney won't be too surprised. He'll manage to get someone else to come for a while. Nobody stays there for long – in fact, I must say you've stuck it out longer than the rest.' He looked at her shrewdly. 'Something's worrying you. Was it that, or something else?'

'It's about Pru – her schooling. I'm concerned about her. She's only just settled down here, and now she'll have to change again. It's bad for her.'

'Not nearly as bad as living in the confined circumstances in which she finds herself just now, in some dump where she hardly sees the only relative she has,' he pointed out tersely, adding in clipped tones, 'And has she settled down as successfully as you would have me believe? It struck me and my committee that the number of days young Pru attended class, and the number of days she didn't, were running pretty well neck and neck.'

Nonie's colour rose at that.

'I'm doing my best for her, aren't I?' she said defensively, angry at his implication of neglect.

'No one is disputing that, little one.' There was, surprisingly, no censure in the level grey eyes. Even the man's voice was noncommittal. 'There are times, however, when even one's best isn't good enough. In your case just let's say it can be improved upon, if you lower that prickly barrier a little and face the thing squarely. Independence – especially the feminine variety – can be quite a tedious commodity if it's overdone.'

'Look, Mr. Lomax–' she flushed angrily – 'is it a job you're offering me, or a lecture? The fact that I've just accepted the one doesn't automatically give you the right to proceed with the other. If you want to know, I find your whole attitude insufferably superior and dictatorial!'

'And I find yours stubborn, headstrong, and not a little immature.' He grinned maddeningly. 'It must be a part of that excessive independence of which I spoke.'

'The *feminine* variety.' She mimicked his own phrase a little acidly. 'What have you against females, Mr. Lomax?'

The grin broadened, and Nonie seethed. The dancing lights in the depths of his wide-spaced eyes under the beetling brows told her that he was enjoying himself.

'Nothing against them at all, collectively,' he replied suavely. 'Indeed they're an admirable invention. Even individually they have their points. You can hardly have failed to notice that I have just given myself the pleasure of conducting one particularly charming and decorative member of the sex as far as the Golf Club, with positively no show of reluctance whatever. I can assure you that had I disapproved I shouldn't have bothered.'

Nonie stood up. 'Come on, Pru!' she called. 'We'll have to get back now, darling.' She turned. 'When do you wish me to go to your brother?' she asked in a tight, formal voice.

'We'll give Barney a week to find someone. I'll speak to him when I take you back just now, and come for you on Sunday. Right?'

'You don't need to take us back. We can walk there ourselves,' she pointed out a little ungraciously.

'But it's my pleasure, Miss Gotthart,' he emphasized, teeth glinting in a smile so smooth and silky and sarcastic that Nonie felt she could have screamed.

'I suspect you doubt my sincerity,' he added, amusement crinkling the lazy grey eyes.

She pressed her lips together and set off, scarcely waiting to make sure that her little sister was following. How this man could pique and annoy! Nonie could only hope that, once she had settled down at the old homestead with his brother and the ex-fiancée, she would see little, or preferably nothing, of Jacey Lomax himself.

Once more she found herself packing up, but this time there was not much work involved. The unattractive black uniforms she had been wearing went back into the staff pool, and her other personal effects were few. A good thing that she had not even opened the stout tin trunk that contained her mother's things. The ornaments and pictures were still wrapped in tissue exactly as she had placed them before leaving Sydney. They would have to remain there for some time yet, she acknowledged, replacing the lid with a sigh, and snapping the brass catches shut once more. Although the trunk would accompany them out to Tuckarimba, the time had not yet arrived to unpack it. That time would not arrive until the old home got back into Nonie's own hands, and since Jacey Lomax had made it clear that he would not consider selling until his brother was well again, it was as much in Nonie's interests as his that Raynor Lomax should make a quick recovery, and that a reconciliation should take place between himself and Ilse.

Nonie's lips quirked ironically. Strange to find herself in complete accord with Jacey Lomax over something, if for differing motives. Yes, he could certainly count on Nonie to do all she could to help Raynor on to his feet once more, although he need not be made too much aware of the underlying reason for her co-operation. Perverse man that he was, it would be just like him to decide not to sell at all if he guessed how much she really wanted that old place!

On the following Friday Nonie went along to the school and waited outside for the children to come out. She had promised Pru that she would be there on the final day, to help the child to carry the extra books and other oddments that she had accumulated in her desk during her months in town.

It was a bright, still day, almost stiflingly still. The sky held the harsh glare of pale heat that Nonie could remember well from her childhood sojourn in this inland climate. It was a dry heat, without the humidity of the coast that she had always found so sticky and trying. Nonie actually enjoyed this beating, dry heat that set the landscape shimmering under a hard, blue sky. She sat on the wall outside the school, bare legs dangling, tapping her heels gently against the bricks in time to the tune she was humming as she waited.

And then she ceased her humming as a long grey car came up the street in her direction. Even at this distance Nonie could recognize the fiery glory of that auburn head in the passenger seat. The driver's identity remained a mystery right to the moment when the shiny vehicle swished past.

Nonie gazed after it, sighed. She might have known it would be Jacey Lomax at the wheel, with the delectable Delphine at his side. The kitten smile had been playing around her red lips as she glanced through the window as they passed, but Nonie doubted if she herself had been recognized by either of them – certainly not by Jacey, anyway. His face had been half hidden beneath the wide slouch hat, and at the speed he was travelling his eyes had doubtless been fastened upon the road.

Just as well he hadn't seen the girlish figure balanced on the wall in the sunshine, or he might have stopped, and Nonie was bound to admit she'd have felt at a distinct disadvantage, barelegged and untidy as she was, beside the beautifully groomed presence of that Delphine woman.

It was the same grey car that called for them on Sunday. It slid into the front yard quietly, so quietly that if Nonie had not been watching from the window she might not even have known it had arrived. She found that her whole body had been stiff and tense, waiting here for this moment.

Somehow she forced herself to relax, gathered up the smaller articles about her, and called to Pru.

'Are you ready?' Jacey Lomax stood in the doorway. If he noticed the whiteness about her mouth, the uncertainty in her strained blue eyes, he didn't comment. 'Where are your cases?'

'There are just the two. And a trunk in the porch.'

Nonie and Pru followed him out into the yard in silence. He stowed the luggage swiftly, heaving the trunk into place with an ease that secretly amazed Nonie. She climbed obediently into the front seat, and Pru scrambled willingly into the back one. Then Jacey Lomax closed the door and took his own place at the wheel.

As they swept around in a circle past the entrance to the dingy building, the pelican danced a final, sad farewell on his creaking hinge. Nonie couldn't stop looking at him, so desolate and despondent did he seem, hopping on his one webbed foot.

'Sorry to be leaving?' Jacey had seen her backward, lingering gaze.

'No, not at all.' She shrugged. 'I was just saying good-bye to the bird. He looks so lonely, somehow. It's an awful place to have to be for the whole of one's life. For him, there's no escape.'

'But for you, yes. I'm glad you see it in a sensible light, and have agreed to come.' He shot her a swift, appraising look, took in the sudden wetness of her thick dark

69

lashes.

'I didn't know pelicans *were* pink,' Nonie heard herself say stupidly, hurriedly, in a husky indistinct voice.

'They're not, as a rule, except for the beak. I doubt if that one was ever pink either, although it's hard to tell underneath all that dust.' A pause. 'In ancient times the pelican was reputed to wound itself with its own beak in order to feed its young with its blood.'

'How – horrible!'

'Not entirely.' His tone was dry. 'In those days it was considered a symbol of selflessness and piety. That pelican dangling over the door back there is just about as much out of his element in that place as you were yourself. Be thankful that he's only a tin one. Do you want to drive?'

'What, this?' Nonie looked askance at the mere suggestion. The gleaming dashboard held almost as many buttons, switches and dials as a full-sized aeroplane.

'You won't – er – feel sick?' There was the suspicion of a humorous gleam in his eye.

'Thank you, no. I took a tablet,' she replied stiffly – then, as she saw the gleam deepening, 'I've no intention of finding myself in that undignified position again, I can assure you.'

'Or of being beholden for my timely assistance either? I get the message. However, far from *you* being beholden to *me*, you're actually doing me a favour by agreeing to come out to Tuckarimba. Just remember that, will you, any time you get to wondering about it.'

Nonie glanced at him curiously. Could he possibly *believe* in what he was saying?

It seemed that he did. There was no teasing glint in the level grey eyes that met hers for an instant, no satirical lift to the corner of his mouth, either. Jacey Lomax appeared quite solemnly convincing – and as inscrutable as the Sphinx.

'Does your brother know we're coming?' she asked, feeling suddenly more apprehensive about the whole thing – suddenly aware, too, of the actual physical nearness of this big, broad man in the car beside her.

For some unaccountable reason, the impact of his nearness was affecting her in a most unpredictable manner. Nonie felt her breath break short, and a tiny shiver ran right through her.

'We're nearly there,' Jacey Lomax told her, evidently – and fortunately – misinterpreting the shiver which hadn't escaped his eagle gaze. 'You needn't be worried. Ray and Ilse are looking forward to having you, and Pru's presence will buck them both up, I'm sure. The nurse left a couple of days ago, and Ilse flew up as soon as she had gone, to take over the running of the place. She asked Hattie to prepare your room. It used to be two rooms at one time, I believe. It's a big one that you can both share.'

'Looking out to the tankstand?'

'You know it?' Jacey Lomax seemed startled.

'No, n-not really.' Colour rushed to her face. How idiotically careless of her to make such an unthinking remark! 'I – we walked around the outside a bit that night,' she lied confusedly. 'There seemed to be what was probably a bedroom facing on to the side verandah.'

'The side *away* from the wattle-tree where I ran into you. Yes, there is.'

She licked dry lips.

'It – it's very kind of Ilse – to have given us a nice big room to ourselves, I mean.'

'There are plenty of rooms in the house, and she's expecting something in return, of course – your support, companionship, understanding, patience. Raynor's not an easy man at times in his present restricted state, and he was against Ilse coming up from the outset. I'm sure you'll manage, though, so don't look so haunted.'

But 'haunted' was what she was feeling at this precise moment, could he but have guessed. Haunted by remembrance, as the big grey car crested the ridge and swept down towards the creek flat. Haunted by nudging memories that jostled for pride of place in her racing mind. Her mother, in a striped apron and canvas shoes, feeding chooks near the water-trough. Her father, Dermot, riding in through the clump of timber with a screwed-up, faded blue gaze that saw beyond the plains and the valley and dreamed of success that somehow never came.

She swallowed.

'Welcome to Tuckarimba,' said Jacey Lomax gently, taking her arm and drawing her out of the car, completely unaware of the irony of his remark.

Welcome *home*, Nonie corrected him under her breath, as in a daze she began to walk slowly over the grass towards the house.

CHAPTER FOUR

ILSE BJORNIG was older than Nonie had expected. There was a completely mature beauty in her serene face that was both striking and somehow sad, at one and the same time. The radiant smile of welcome with which she received Jacey Lomax couldn't quite disguise the lines of strain about her controlled mouth once the smile had disappeared again, and Nonie couldn't help noticing the momentary anguish in her pale blue eyes as she glanced swiftly behind her, just once and only fleetingly, at the man whom she had left in his wheelchair on the verandah, before coming down the shallow steps to meet them.

Jacey Lomax raised his broad-brimmed hat, and somewhat to Nonie's astonishment kissed this quietly beautiful woman upon her smooth, tanned cheek. Nonie would not have imagined him to be the sort to bestow that particular kind of kiss at all! One didn't associate tall, tanned, forceful 'don't-fence-me-in' fellers with the nonchalant air of polished gallantry displayed by Jacey Lomax just now in greeting the woman who might one day become his sister-in-law.

'How is he, Ilse?'

'A little depressed. I think your new arrivals are going to do him the world of good, though.'

'I hope so.' Jacey still held his wide felt hat in his hand. 'This is Miss Wenona Gotthart, Ilse – Nonie to her friends –' the grey eyes glinted – 'and here – ' with his free hand reaching out and grasping the mercurial Pru – 'is her little sister.'

Ilse smiled gently down at Pru, held out a hand to Nonie.

'Pru, Nonie – I am so glad you've come. We must get your things inside, and then we can set about getting to know each other. But first you must come and meet Ray, since he can't come down here to you.'

Another of those swift, anxious glances in the direction of the verandah.

'You take them up then, Ilse. I'll get the gear.'

Nonie followed the other two up the steps and through the gauze door at the top. There was a dreamlike unreality about this homecoming of hers that left her too bewildered to do more than obey Jacey Lomax's suggestion mechanically. It was all so very different from the way she had imagined her return to Tuckarimba might be. Instead of the quiet thrill of rediscovery alone with little Pru, she found herself being ushered into her own house – the very place in which she had been born! – with the formality of a guest and a stranger. Now she had to hide the conflicting emotions of the moment, and walk up to greet the gaunt, pallid invalid who was wheeling himself impatiently towards her, as if this particular civility was the only thing in her mind at this minute.

'How do you do.'

Raynor Lomax was quite unlike his brother – fairer hair, a nose that was wider, less hawk-like, and a noticeably milder manner. It was difficult to compare his stature, because of the wheel-chair, but by the look of those long, helpless legs it was a fair guess that he would have had much the same impressive physique had he been able to stand upright.

Instead of standing, though, he could only lean forward to spike Pru's hair into further disarray, treating her at the same time to a grin that was sudden, and surprisingly amiable.

'Hello, scrap. Excuse me for not getting up to meet you.'

'Hullo.'

'Come here and let's have a look at you, since we're going to be playmates.'

Pru stepped nearer, and put one finger on the arm of the chair.

'You can't play with me in that,' she told him uncompromisingly, running her gimlet eyes disparagingly over his cumbersome prison.

'Pru!'

Nonie was agonized, her cheeks hot with embarrassment at her young sister's lack of tact. It wasn't as though she hadn't been well warned, either!

'It's all right,' Raynor Lomax's amused voice interpolated. 'I understand kids, and they understand me. Besides—' here a meaning look that was obviously directed towards Ilse – 'I prefer directness. The honest approach is most refreshing, and somewhat unfamiliar these days.'

Pru, bless her, seemed to be the only one amongst them who remained unaware of the general tension this remark had created.

'What's that thing for?' she asked.

'That's the brake.'

'And that?'

'That goes back and fore to turn the wheels. See?'

'Can I do it, d'you think?'

'Have a go if you like. Or, better still, you can push me from behind if I release the brake first. Now.'

'Like that?'

'That's it. You can give me a ride right down the verandah and back if you want to.'

'I'll just go and see about our things, if you'll excuse me,' murmured Nonie, secretly marvelling at the suddenness of the rapport which had sprung up between her unpredictable little sister and the invalid brother whom Jacey had described as 'often difficult'.

Ilse, too, seemed happy to leave the situation as it was.

75

'And if you'll excuse me for a moment too, I'd better see what Hattie is doing about the evening meal.'

Still dazed, Nonie stepped into the hall. It took a few moments for her eyes to become accustomed to the dim interior after the harsh glare of light on the veranda. When she could see properly, the milestones of memory emerged one after another from the shadows. Here was the same oak bench seat along one wall, with a wobbly lid that lifted off to reveal a zinc-lined interior. Beside it was a stand full of polo clubs that must be Raynor's, but the long mirror on the opposite side was where it had always been, too. So was the tall-backed rush chair in the corner. Nonie remembered asking her mother why they weren't taking it with them, for it had long been a family favourite, and her mother had brushed the question aside, taking trouble instead to lift the mirror off its hook and showing Nonie the faded patch on the wall behind it.

'We must leave *some* things for the people who come after us, Nonie,' she had temporized, and in the end there had just been the trunk full of small, more personal items, plus their few suitcases of clothing.

She ran her fingers along the oak seat, sat down in it, mindlessly. After a while she stood up again, walked over to the mirror, moistened her lips and inspected her reflection.

Strange to be looking at the wide-eyed, pale reflection of a young woman's face, when what you actually felt you should be seeing was the plump, jolly, round-cheeked image of a pigtailed eight-year-old. That was what she had always seen in that particular mirror before.

Nonie pushed her blonde hair back behind her ears and gazed at herself critically. She wasn't a person at all right now, she decided objectively, just a bundle of piquant memories that jostled each other for position in a nostalgia that was half pleasant, half painful.

Well, wasn't it what she should have expected, this

feeling of dual personality which had taken possession of her? Wasn't it what she had prepared herself to face, half anticipating, half dreading? One couldn't step back into the past without being very much aware of the experience, especially after all these years spent in yearning to recapture it.

Nonie walked away from the mirror, through the other door, turned left and into the bedroom. Their cases had already been deposited on the floor near one window, and Pru's coat and school beret lay on one of the beds.

She put her handbag on the dressing-table, and looked around her. The proportions of the room were unfamiliar, yet vaguely reminiscent of the place as she had known it. A ridge of plaster above her head soon told her why. This must be where the partition had been. As Jacey Lomax had already told her, two rooms had been knocked into one, to make a pleasantly large and spacious bed-sitting apartment which stretched the entire width of the west wing of the house. Yes, now she had it! That was where one door had been, and the door to the other room had opened from the veranda. In actual fact, she was now standing at the window of what had once been her very own, smaller bedroom.

Nonie wandered to the other window, the one away from the tankstand.

From here you could see right down over the creek flats to the river itself. There was the engine-shed, behind the oleanders, and a little beyond that the windmill. Between the two wound the path up which they had carried the shrouded form of her father on that fateful day. Nonie hadn't realized at the time just what it was that they were doing, but she had known from the conversations going on about her, and her mother's ill-concealed consternation, that something dramatic and irrevocable had happened, and it was from this very window that she had watched the mysterious procession approach. She had

77

never seen her father again, and it wasn't very long after that that her mother had broken the news to her that they would have to leave Tuckarimba for good.

Nonie remembered that bleak moment very well indeed.

Thinking about it now – but with the implications of old Bundy's revelations ringing in her head – she felt weakness assailing her limbs. A dew was breaking over her forehead, and there was a sudden, painful swelling in her throat. Had Dermot really felt so hopeless about the future that he had simply chosen not to have a future at all? Had he cared about them, her mother and herself? *Really* cared, that is? Had he loved them, even if he couldn't find it in him to love this place?

Nonie clenched her hands together. She would never know the answer, and maybe it was better that she shouldn't. Yet it was with complete, despairing honesty that she admitted that the answer suddenly mattered in a way that she could not have been expected to anticipate. It mattered because she was *here*. With absolute clarity she knew now that she should not have come back. Not ever.

It would have been better for everyone if she had never happened to run into the old mailman at all. Then the pungent, bitter-sweet memories would not be haunting her, crushing her, now – because she wouldn't have got the idea of coming back at all, would she? It was typical of her, this, wasn't it? She had always been inclined to be too impetuous, headstrong. This time it hadn't paid off, that impulsiveness of hers.

She had fooled herself, telling herself that it was the answer for her and Pru, the solution to everything. It hadn't been so far, and it wouldn't be now. It hadn't been the right thing to do. What had it brought them but tension and strain and enforced breaks in Pru's schooling, and even more uncertainty about their future than they had had back there in the city?

She had done the *wrong thing*, and in this moment of acknowledging it, Nonie felt more wretched, more alone, than she had ever done in her entire life.

'What is it?'

Jacey Lomax's voice came from the doorway, and she turned instantly to see him standing just inside the room with the tin trunk tilted upon one broad shoulder.

'What's up?' he asked again, putting down the trunk with little effort, and crossing the room to where she was standing.

'I'm tired, that's all.' Nonie pulled a wry face, moved back from the window.

'No, it's more than that.' His presence checked her. 'Look at me,' he commanded. Already his fingers were tipping her chin.

'It's more than that,' Jacey Lomax stated again, quite positively. 'You look – tortured over something. What's the matter?'

'Nothing that time and a good night's sleep won't cure,' she returned briskly. 'Thanks for bringing in the trunk.'

For a moment she wondered if he was going to argue the point, but instead he merely shrugged. Then he went over to the window, leaned both hands upon the sill and stared out at the very same view at which she herself had just been looking. He appeared not to see the view, though. Not consciously, anyway. He seemed almost absent-minded, screwing up his eyes into slits in the brownness of his face as he studied the sun-drenched distances abstractedly, almost as if he wasn't seeing them at all.

Nonie saw the muscles in his tanned forearms rippling as he flexed his fingers against the ledge. Then he stretched to his full height once more. The wide shoulders squared themselves, and he turned around and fastened her with a curiously impersonal look.

'You've probably realized that the house is in a much, much worse condition than you'd have been led to believe on your brief inspection of the outside that evening in the dark,' he said levelly. 'A good deal of money would need to be spent to get the old place into reasonable order if one were intending to reside here permanently. Is that what's worrying you?'

She shook her head a little stupidly, trying to take in what he was saying.

'I only stayed here for a short time,' he continued, 'while my own place was being got ready. But it was long enough to be aware of the shortcomings. I put a lot of the old junk out in the boxroom behind the kitchen quarters, and that did something to improve the look of general dereliction. Without all those bits and pieces lying around it does look a little bit better, and we can go through them and burn most of them before a new owner takes over, but I realize that there's still a basic problem, a structural one, of some magnitude.'

'It's not that at all, Mr. Lomax.'

'Because if it is—' he paused, inspected the toe of his elastic-sided stockman's boot as if it held some momentary but absorbing interest for him – 'if it *is*, then I'm sure that something can be arranged, when and if the time comes, some adjustment—'

Nonie shook her head again.

'It's nothing like that,' she muttered huskily, cursing the treacherous tremor in her voice. What a fool he would think her if she confessed now that she wasn't interested in buying the house after all! What an abject, stupid, shilly-shallying little fool!

'The price I quoted to you was merely a guide, you know. I hadn't really made up my mind. You mustn't let it bother you too much for the present. Don't meet troubles half-way.'

Half-way!

Half-way, the man said! Little did he realize that she wasn't a mere half-way to trouble, but – thanks entirely to her own rash actions – up to her very neck in the stuff.

'It is not *anything* like that,' she stressed again, with rather desperate firmness.

'What, then?'

He asked it in a way that *invited* an answer. He was standing very near now, and his voice had deepened in a way that was gentle yet compelling, and in his grey eyes was an expression that undoubtedly communicated sympathy, that tempted the telling of one's confidences.

There was also a certain rocklike quality in the man's stance, a steadfastness in the unflickering greyness of his faintly speculative gaze, that threatened Nonie's resolution altogether just then. She had a sudden, quite shocking urge to fling herself against the broad khaki chest that blocked her escape, confess the predicament into which she had got herself and Pru, and beg for a little sensible, objective, *male* advice. Those sinewy arms could be quite comforting in moments of distress, she had found that much out from previous experience.

Horrified at the trend of her own thoughts, Nonie drew back hastily, concealing her inward dismay.

'Mr. Lomax, the fact that you are now my employer hardly gives you the right to probe so persistently into my personal affairs, I think.'

How cold and discouraging that sounded! Even more cold and discouraging than she had intended it to be, but she was still in a state of dire alarm at the turmoil of her own thoughts and emotions, not to mention the direction that they had just taken!

'Forgive me if I've spoken rather bluntly,' she added, less certainly.

'But wasn't that just what you *meant* to be, Miss Gotthart – blunt?' His own voice was chillier than she could have imagined possible, and the warmth had drained from his eyes, leaving them flinty as a sabre's steel, and as coldly penetrating. 'Why apologise, when you meant exactly what you said? Honesty is always more preferable than either hypocrisy or false remorse, after all.' A pause. 'I take it – or may I? – that you have no intention of going back on your word about coming here, about staying here with Ilse and Raynor, at least for a while, even though the prospect appears to have rather *thrown* you in some strange way.'

Nonie's chin went up. 'It hasn't thrown me at all,' she assured him tartly, stung by his tone. 'I have every intention of keeping to the arrangement we agreed, for however long you feel I may be needed here.'

'And—?'

'And what?'

'After that?'

She looked up, startled, recovered swiftly.

'After that,' she stated calmly, 'I shall see. Haven't you just been telling me yourself, it's a mistake to meet trouble half-way?'

'Touché.' There was the faintest lift to the corner of the levelled mouth. 'In that case, there's little more to be said at the moment, is there? If you'll excuse me, I'll leave you to get on with your unpacking.'

She didn't turn, even when she heard the crisp staccato sound of his boots crossing the pinewood floor to the door. She just went on standing there, numb and wooden.

In the hall came Ilse's voice.

'You'll stay and eat with us, Jacey.'

'No, Ilse, thanks. Not tonight.'

'But I thought—'

'Something's cropped up – I'm sorry, my dear. Give Hattie my apologies if I've disappointed her.'

'When will we see you, then?'

'I'll look by tomorrow if I can.'

Nonie took Pru's beret and coat off the bed, hung up

the coat on the hook behind the door and threw the beret in the top shelf of the wardrobe. She eyed the tin trunk with misgiving, decided not to unpack it at all. Not just yet, anyway. Maybe this confusing welter of emotions might sort themselves out if she gave herself time, and then she would know more clearly what to do. At present she'd better leave things as they were. The contents of that particular case had been there long enough already, so it wasn't going to make much difference to their condition whether they remained a few weeks, or even months, longer, anyway.

Nonie found the key in her handbag, unlocked the padlock that held the metal clasp in place, and lifted out the few bits of clothing that she had placed on the very top for want of room anywhere else. A couple of light jerseys, too warm for just now, but they would need a press to steam the creases out. Two shirts that Pru would need for school, and a pair of sandshoes that she had pushed down the side.

Back at the window again, she could see that the light was fading. Night gave little warning of its approach. It just dropped a soft grey blanket over the hills, swamped the last faint rose flush from the western sky, and then the stars sprang out, one after another. The Evening Star. Hesperus, big and bright and single, over there above the pump-shed. Glowing and blinking in solitary splendour. Then, as the colour ebbed from the sky altogether, there was suddenly a myriad of them, sprinklings and scatterings of stars, all over the heavens. Constellations of them – the Giant Saucepan, the Southern Cross, all shimmering and winking over the still night-time hush of the Australian bush.

Nonie sighed. If only she could find the same peace within herself as that great, still tranquillity outside, everything could have been just perfect. But it wasn't perfect at all, was it. Far from it. It had been a mistake to think that she could ignore the bad bits and recapture only the happy moments in coming back here. With a new and adult understanding she was aware that her memories had been a child's memories, whereas now she was a woman, with enough experience of the rawness of life to know that things were never as Utopian as a child's eye view would have them be. Children were apt to over-simplify. Life was full of ups and downs, and just as she herself had always done her best to cushion Pru against the 'downs', her parents had probably done exactly the same with her. Children had a right to be happy, didn't they, because as you got older, complications were bound to set in – things like lack of money, and finding congenial work, and getting on with people for whom you seemed to have a built-in antipathy. Like Jason Lomax, for instance. She just couldn't seem to be with him for two minutes on end before they were striking sparks off each other. Each time they met she was determined to remain civil, to hide the irritation that his authoritarian manner aroused in her – and each time she was unsuccessful. It always seemed to finish in the same way, with her having to reassert her independence, maintain her rights as an individual.

Nonie found him a disturbing person altogether, for even while she recognized him as autocratic and over-bearing, she had to admit that there was a sort of magnetism about the man that was hard to resist. Yet resist she must and would! With *that* sort of man you had to, didn't you, or before you knew where you were he'd be ruling your life, jerking the strings to make you dance, like he did with all of those human puppets of his. Nonie had the idea that Ilse and Ray were two of the puppets, perhaps unwilling ones, and Pru would do almost any-thing for Jacey Lomax. She, Nonie, wasn't going to be a puppet too, and the sooner he accepted that fact, the better.

She wasn't at all sure – and it would be all to the good if she were proved right in this! – that Raynor was going to be as difficult to handle as his brother had said, in spite of Jacey's warning on that score.

When she went back to the verandah he was playing draughts with Pru, and the two of them were laughing softly over a move that he had apparently missed.

'I'm out of practice.' Raynor Lomax snapped his fingers, chuckling. 'What a fool, not to see that you'd get that second one.'

'Do sit down, Wenona.' Ilse put down the piece of tapestry she had been doing, and indicated one of the cane chairs that were strewn haphazardly about the verandah. 'Mind that loose board, do. I really must get one of the men to fix it for me.'

'You see, I am completely useless, and therefore can't,' Raynor Lomax stated, with what seemed unnecessary venom.

Ilse flushed. 'I didn't mean that, Ray, and you know it,' she said quietly. 'I didn't even mean for Jacey to do it. One of the station hands could easily put a new piece of wood in for me, or even the blacksmith if I asked him, I'm sure.'

'Would you like a drink, Nonie? You don't mind us calling you that? It's going to be hard not to, since Pru does it all the time.'

'But of course. I hope you will.'

Raynor had wheeled himself over to a cabinet upon which stood an array of bottles, an ice-bucket, and a jug of orange juice.

'Just orange, please, then. Is it fresh? How lovely!'

'We've been hearing all about you from Pru.' He passed her a glass. 'It came as a bit of a surprise to hear that you'd been actually thinking of buying this place. Jacey had omitted to mention it, for some strange reason.'

Nonie bit her lip, vexed that Pru had unwittingly said

something already that she'd hoped she wouldn't.

'We did look at it,' she admitted as calmly as she could, 'but that's as far as things had got. In any case, it's not for sale at present anyway, is it, so I'd sort of shelved the matter in my own mind for just now.'

'Hm. Well, I hope for my sake as well as yours it's not going to have to be shelved for too long. Not that it wasn't decent of Jacey to make it available. I was going slowly out of my mind down there in the city – doctors and nurses pushing and pummelling at one from morning till night. Visiting hours under restriction, meal hours, bells going all the time – no peace, no privacy. I can tell you it was a relief to get away, and it was a red-letter day when Jacey sent that meddlesome nurse away from here, too, even if it does mean putting up with these tiresome sessions of Ilse's instead.'

'It's only twice a day, darling, and it's always progress when the physiotherapist ousts the nurse, remember,' Ilse reproved him lightly. 'Whatever makes you want to come to a place like this, though, Nonie? You're young and gay, you should be down there in the bright lights, in the centre of things, instead of tucked away out here in the country, shouldn't you?'

'Me an' Nonie *love* the country,' chimed in Pru reproachfully. 'We've been in the city and it wasn't all that much fun. Bossy old landladies and everyone telling you where to go and where not to go all the time, and nowhere to play and not much to do. We're going to *love* it here. I do already – don't you, Nonie?' Her thin face was glowing with enthusiasm. 'I've been doing lots of exploring already, and it's just like you said it'd be, Nonie. Just.'

'Well, at least you'll have had a chance to live in the place, and if Jacey does ever decide to put it on the market again, you'll know all the shortcomings. Not many would-be purchasers have the chance of a trial run first. You'll be able to recite all the drawbacks, and beat him down,' Raynor pointed out somewhat flippantly.

'Ray! What a thing to say.'

'Well, so she will. You know as well as I do, Ilse, that the place is practically falling apart. Anyway, it'd do Jacey the world of good to be beaten down by someone, to meet his match just for once.'

Nonie couldn't resist exchanging smiles with him. She was beginning to warm to Raynor Lomax. They appeared to agree basically over at least one essential point, and that was brother Jacey's almost unbearable domination. On the other hand, she had already developed a sneaking sympathy for Ilse. Gentle Ilse. Those barbed remarks and pointed jibes of Raynor's were undoubtedly intended for her, and they mostly reached their target, too. They must have been particularly hurtful, and yet Ilse accepted them with calm and dignity, successfully concealing her true feelings. In fact, had not Jacey already put Nonie in the picture she would have found it hard to believe that these two had actually been engaged to be married at the time of Raynor's accident. One didn't intentionally set out to hurt the very person whom one loved, surely – and yet Raynor's remarks were cruelly calculated to do just that to Ilse. Just as if he were punishing her for something.

Poor Ilse.

And poor Raynor too. There was a trapped, restless look about him as he sat there in his wheelchair. For such an intelligent and previously athletic man it must be a prison indeed! Perhaps sheer frustration drove him to wound Ilse in this way.

When Hattie called from the end of the verandah they all went in for tea. Or dinner, as it turned out to be.

Nonie, hungry by now, found herself more than ready for the delicious roast of mutton that was set in front of Raynor, with vegetable dishes in accompaniment, holding peas and cauliflower, and a sauceboat of rich gravy. The apricot pie which followed was nothing short of a culinary work of art. Eyeing its flaky, shiny top, decorated with small pastry leaves and a twining border, Nonie was already having secret misgivings as to how she was going to take Hattie's place in the kitchen when that lady was having one of her week-ends off. She hadn't tried to conceal her lack of experience from Jacey Lomax, but he had paid scarcely any attention to her protestations, all the same. Now she was quite sure that she would make a fool of herself when the time came, and she didn't exactly relish the prospect. Nonie inspected the pie with even greater attention, wondering dubiously if she could ever produce one something like it. A good thing if she could, since it was obviously popular with this particular household, and after second helpings all round there was only one wedge left – for Hattie herself.

Later Nonie excused herself and Pru.

'Yes, you'll want to unpack properly, I'm sure, and have a proper night's rest.' Ilse was immediately understanding. 'Jacey said you certainly weren't getting much peace in that place you were in in town – I forget what he called it. By the way, if you want a bath the chip-heater is lit. It's a bit archaic, but it does get results. I'm sure you'll manage.'

'We'll manage all right, thank you, Ilse. Good night. Good night – er – Raynor.'

She followed her sister in the direction of the hall, then across it, to their room.

Archaic it might be, but Nonie found the bathroom – it was a wash-house, really, with a cement floor and laundry tubs at one end of it – a comfortingly familiar place. It didn't have the acutely painful associations of the view from their enlarged bedroom window, anyway, and that was a comfort. She must not get back to thinking about *that*, however, or let the present uncertainties and doubts make her more tired and depressed than she already was. Enough to acknowledge that she had been wrong to come, and leave it at that.

The trouble so far as that particular line of thought was concerned was that it, too, led to an unsatisfactory conclusion. Pru herself was the conclusion! It did look as though Pru, in her childish and innocent excitement, was already regarding Tuckarimba as her future home. Already it obviously held for her the same uncomplicated delights and charms that it had once upon a time held for Nonie. At eight, you didn't see the drawbacks. You weren't aware of the undercurrents, and you *certainly* didn't appreciate the difficulties inherent in living so near a man like Jacey Lomax! Right under his eagle, and interfering, eye!

From the darkness of the verandah, once she had tucked Pru in and heard her prayers, Nonie could see the oblong row of lights that must be the windows of the new Tuckarimba homestead. They lay well above the level of her own eyes, half-way up the hillside where the house crouched in its sentinel position at the head of the valley. Nonie could just distinguish dark figures moving about against the light. Soon after that, another light blinked on a little way from the main building, and after that came the noise of a car's engine revving up. The sound seemed to slice through the night, reverberating around the valley before finding itself hemmed in by the hills and thrown back upon itself from their rugged barriers.

Presently the twin shafts of headlamps' beams swept the road and Nonie backed almost instinctively, cursing herself for a fool as her heart's beat increased its rate. Why be frightened, when he couldn't possibly see her or know that she was here, a slender pyjama-clad figure in the darkness behind the gauze?

He wasn't coming in, in any case, because the sleek car now raced on, down the track beyond the sprawl of the original homestead, in the direction of Whalebone Crossing and the town. Jacey Lomax obviously had other fish to fry tonight. Nonie had a feeling, though, that whatever it was that had 'cropped up' it had been of his own on-the-spot invention, which he was now converting into fact.

For a long while after that, Nonie lay in the darkness, unable to get to sleep. Finally she got up again, pulled on her seersucker wrap without even bothering to tie it in place, and trod silently back to the verandah.

If only she could sort herself out! For the present, of course, she had to remain where she was, because an undertaking was an undertaking. It was *afterwards* that worried her now. Should she carry on with what she could at last see had been an extraordinarily ill-conceived idea, or abandon the entire notion and go back to Sydney?

The place here was certainly in shocking repair. After a down-payment on it there would be obvious repairs required that couldn't possibly wait for very much longer. Jacey Lomax had no intention, naturally enough, of throwing good money after bad on this crumbling edifice. He was a businessman, not a sentimentalist. *Certainly* not a sentimentalist! The repairs would be up to Nonie, and she couldn't see herself left with nearly enough capital to get her market garden going, let alone buy her little van. Without transport, the thing wouldn't be viable at all, so even supposing that she could overcome the disappointment of her personal reaction to these reawakened and painful memories, it was extremely doubtful if she could ever get the venture off the ground.

Unless, perhaps, Jacey were to make some 'adjustment'.

Out of the question. Nonie couldn't bear to be beholden to a man like that, not even for a *small* adjustment, and it looked as though she'd need a very large one indeed if she were to carry out her former plans.

Easy enough, the decision, if it were only for herself. But the awful thing was that Pru liked it here. *Loved* it here. She wanted to stay. Indeed, so far as Pru was concerned they had arrived at the end of the road, they had reached their Shangri-la. To turn back now? How could she possibly justify such a contradictory action to her little sister? She'd think her quite, quite crazy. She'd think she'd taken leave of her senses, and in fact Nonie was beginning to wonder if perhaps she hadn't done just that!

'Couldn't you sleep either?' Raynor's voice came from the other end of the verandah.

Nonie, glancing along that way, startled, saw that he too was in his pyjamas, having just wheeled himself around the corner. He was sitting in his chair, smoking a cigarette.

'It's because you're in strange surroundings,' he added with unconscious irony, as she approached rather timidly. 'It often works that way.'

'Yes, you're probably right. What about you, though, Mr.—?'

'Raynor. Why hesitate? Your little sister says it already.'

'Are – are you in pain?' she suggested, a little uncertainly.

His crisp directness of speech had reminded her a little bit of his brother just now, and it had the effect of disconcerting her.

Raynor Lomax grimaced.

'A little. Ilse tells me it's a healthy sign. For too long I didn't feel anything, so maybe there's something in what she says.'

'I'm sure there must be. I think Ilse is a – a sweet person.'

91

'Do you now?' He studied her with interest. 'That's a snap judgment, surely. Or has Jacey been extolling her virtues in advance, by any chance?'

'What an odd thing to say.' She seated herself in one of the substantial cane chairs, drawing her wrap about her and wondering at the sudden bitterness in his tone. 'I'm a good judge of character on my own account,' she added firmly.

'Hmm.' Raynor shifted his position. 'What would you say about *me*, then? Let's hear the worst.'

'You? Why, I hardly know you!'

'You know me as well as you know Ilse,' he pointed out logically. 'Come on, Miss Good-Judge-of-Character. You must have formed some opinion, so let's have it.'

Nonie was tongue-tied. She was wishing now that she had never got herself involved in this strange, nocturnal conversation with the enigmatic Raynor Lomax.

'Would you say I'm, for instance, a *reasonable* man?' he insisted, and she could see his mouth twisting in amusement at his own question.

'Except when you're busy enjoying yourself by baiting people who you know are already at a disadvantage and can't answer back.'

'Meaning you?'

'Meaning me. You know perfectly well that I am in your brother's employment, and I've no intention of involving myself in an analysis of the family's personalities on my very first evening here.'

'You mean you need more time?'

'I mean not now, not ever,' she replied crisply. 'It – it wouldn't be proper.'

'What you're trying to say is, Jacey wouldn't like it,' he elaborated for her slyly. 'That's Jacey, spoiling things as usual.'

'Is that fair, Raynor? I should think you should be grateful to Mr. Lomax.'

'Grateful!'

'Well – I mean—' she floundered helplessly – 'I suppose he took a lot of trouble, arranging for you and Ilse to come back here. And he meant it for the best, getting *us* here, too.'

'I suppose he did,' agreed Raynor, surprisingly gently. 'I'm not getting at *you*, child, or your kid sister, either. I was genuinely glad when he said you were coming. I've already told you that, and it's the truth. Ilse and I were getting on each other's nerves, and you'll be company and a welcome distraction. That's what you're being right this minute, Nonie. But don't talk to me about gratitude in connection with anything Jacey does, Nonie, or you'll be making a very big initial mistake. That brother of mine never makes any decision without a reason – and that reason is never one that doesn't suit his own particular book, you can take it from me.'

Nonie wiggled her bare toes and watched them expressionlessly. She had no intention of being drawn into any form of comment where Jacey Lomax was concerned, even though, silently, she half agreed.

'Careful little creature, aren't you?' Raynor's teeth glinted in the dim verandah light. He changed tack. 'That's an enchanting young sister you've got, and no mistake. We're going to be friends, she and I, I can tell.'

'I hope you will be. Pru loves it here already.'

'She lacks your cautious approach.'

'I'm not always cautious,' Nonie replied candidly, adding a little bitterly, 'Sometimes I'm far too impetuous for our own good, hers and mine, I'm afraid.'

'Like landing yourself in that Pink Pelican place in town? Jacey told us about that. He reckoned you'd be better out of it, I gather.'

Nonie licked her lips. 'Is – was that partly why he got us here?'

Raynor shrugged carelessly. 'Who knows why Jacey

93

does things? Even if you asked him, he wouldn't tell you. Jacey never does. Jacey never explains his actions to anyone, it's almost a principle with him.'

'Maybe that's the sort of principle that can rebound on one,' Nonie said wisely. 'Maybe one's actions can be misinterpreted sometimes if one just doesn't bother to explain them, wouldn't you think?'

'Hmm.' A pause. 'Perhaps you think I'm tough on him, with what I've just been saying.'

'You sounded as if you meant it.'

'You consider me bitter, don't you? Bitter, and a little unfair?'

'I'm thinking this is the strangest conversation to be having in the middle of the night with someone I scarcely know,' she told him evasively. 'And I can't see where it's getting either of us. What I think doesn't matter in the slightest. If you're being unfair to anyone, you'll know it yourself, won't you? As for being bitter, I can understand that you must feel terribly resentful and frustrated not being able to get about in the way that you used to.'

'Can you? Can you really understand that?' Raynor studied her earnest face thoughtfully. 'Yes, I believe you really can, my dear. You have a sensitive, imaginative little face, and a capacity for feeling and caring about other people.' He reached out a hand, touched the side of her cheek gently. 'I think you're going to be good for us all, do you know that, Nonie?'

The satire had died from his face, the smoothly ironic tone from his voice. Raynor had spoken with a sort of quiet wonder that touched Nonie to the very core. It was the first time in their brief acquaintance that she knew him to be completely sincere in what he was saying, and his sincerity had been about *her*.

Pity stirred in her. Pity for this big, restless, bitter man confined so despairingly to his wheel-chair. Pity for the gentle Ilse whom he seemed bent upon wounding with his barbed repartee, and who obviously loved him enough to suffer his churlish treatment with what amounted to almost saintly patience.

She longed, then, to help them all in whatever way she could, although she couldn't see how her own presence could make much difference. Maybe Pru's would, though. Because Jacey Lomax had told her that his brother loved children, and this at least was true.

'I hope so, Raynor. I hope we'll be good for everyone,' she said a little huskily. She stood up abruptly. 'If you'll excuse me now, I think I'll go to bed after all.'

'Sleep well, Nonie. And I think I shall, too – better than I'd been going to, anyway. Good night.'

'Good night.'

Nonie watched him turn his chair and wheel it off around the corner again. Then she padded barefoot back along the verandah to the entrance to her own room and went inside.

CHAPTER FIVE

It was a long time before Nonie fell asleep that night, and when she woke up she found that the sun was well up in the sky. Glancing at the clock, she was horrified to find that it was almost eleven o'clock. Eleven! And no one had been to waken her, or even to see where she was and why she had not yet appeared.

She had a quick shower in the yellowish water that was pumped up to the homestead from the creek – cold water today, since the geyser had not been lit. Indeed, the ashes could be seen lying in a depressing little heap at the base of the cylinder.

Nonie dressed hastily, then cleaned out the fireplace, went kitchenwards to seek out some paper and kindlings to re-set it. There she made the acquaintance of Hattie, a thin sparrow of a creature with critical black eyes beneath a frizzy mop of wiry greying curls. Hattie appeared quick and active and extremely efficient. She showed Nonie where the kindlers were stacked, then went out the back door with a basket full of dish-towels and drying cloths which she had been boiling in a pan on top of the big black cooking range.

No one else seemed to be around this morning. It was only when she stepped out through the hall to the front of the house that Nonie found out why. On the verandah there appeared to be a morning-tea party in full progress. Ilse was presiding over a trolley upon which lay an assortment of cheeses and biscuits, plain white cups and saucers, and a large brown enamel tea-pot. Raynor's chair was strategically placed near a small wicker table, and in a canvas deck-lounger beside him sprawled the long-legged figure of Jacey Lomax. On the other lounger, twin

96

to Jacey's, reclined the decorative Delphine Simpson. The fiery splendour of her rich auburn hair was complemented perfectly by the unrelieved white of the simple tennis dress she was wearing. Her shapely legs in their short white ankle-socks and canvas shoes were crossed in a way that accentuated the rounded curves of her body. From one hand she was dangling a pair of extravagantly-framed sunglasses, while the other reached idly for a Sao biscuit from the plate on Ilse's trolley. She was just about to bite into the dry cracker with her neat white even teeth when those long lynx-green eyes caught sight of Nonie, poised uncertainly in the hall doorway.

'Why, Jacey darling, look who's here. Your little protegée in the flesh.' The tones were husky, slowly amused.

Everyone in the gathering turned then to look at the object of Delphine's remark.

'Ah, Nonie, do come and join us in a cup of tea.' That was Ilse's voice, tranquil and kind.

'Miss Gotthart.' Jacey's own deep murmur of acknowledgment just reached her as he drew up his long legs and scrambled lazily to his feet.

'Oh, please – don't anybody get up—' but her embarrassed protest came too late, of course, for Jacey Lomax was already hooking his elastic-sided boot beneath another chair, drawing it nearer and indicating that she should sit in it.

'I'm afraid I'm disturbing everyone,' she muttered apologetically.

'Not me, you'll have noticed, and I don't intend that you should. I'm conserving all my energies for tennis later.' Delphine popped the last piece of biscuit into her mouth, and passed Ilse her cup. 'Some more if it's there, please, Ilse. I've such a dry throat this morning. It must have been that smoky atmosphere in the Club last night.'

'Why go there, then?' Raynor spoke for the first time, sliding one of his blatantly cynical looks at Delphine's pouting mouth.

'Because, darling, I was asked to go there. Asked in a way that made it quite difficult to refuse, and by a man who, in spite of his indisputable charm in many directions, doesn't like to take no for an answer.'

'Jacey, I suppose.' Raynor's scowling gaze dwelt disapprovingly upon his tea-cup.

'Who else?' agreed Delphine sweetly. 'Although it's perhaps hardly flattering to him that you recognized my definition of your dictatorial brother quite so promptly. Why shouldn't I whisk him away sometimes? You don't have any objections, do you, Raynor? I should think you'd have been quite pleased, actually.'

'And what do you mean by that?'

'Well –' slim shoulders shrugged a little deprecatingly – 'I just thought you *should* be, that's all. If his attention's on me, then it can't be anywhere else, can it? I thought you'd welcome a little – um – timely diversion for Jacey's attentions just now, if you follow me.'

'Stop it, Delphine.' Jacey spoke with lazy authority. 'Just because I've agreed to drive you over to this crazy tennis party of yours it doesn't give you the right to start talking in riddles and innuendoes, especially at this hour of the day. Drink up your tea, and we'll get going.'

'It's not a riddle to Raynor, though. *He* understands me, don't you, Ray?' She slid him an oblique look from beneath her long lashes, then pouted back at his brother. 'Anyway, I can't think why you won't stay and play tennis yourself, Jacey. You were invited too, you know. It's not very fair just taking me over and dumping me, like a piece of unwanted baggage.' Her tone dropped to a wheedling softness, to which Jacey Lomax seemed completely impervious. Or was he? Just for a moment Nonie could have sworn that his firm lips were threatening to curve uncontrollably. Instead they pronounced with inscrutable solemnity—

'A piece of baggage, certainly. The "unwanted" bit is obviously thrown in as a challenge, but I refuse to be goaded, Delphine.' He got to his feet, scooped his broad-brimmed hat off the table. 'Come on, then, we'll go.'

'Why *won't* you stay the whole day, Jacey?' she persisted, getting up and putting her cup back on the tray near Ilse. 'It would do you good to relax for a while. You can be much too serious at times, my pet. I suppose you're going off instead on some of that horrid business of yours, as usual.'

This time his lips did twitch.

'That's perfectly correct. And I reckon it'll be time better spent than hitting lollipops over the net to you girls.'

'Dear Jacey! Now you're being humble, which is *quite* out of character, since we all know you can produce the most devastating drives when you like.' Delphine replaced her sunglasses on her pretty freckled nose and followed him towards the gauze door which led to the front steps. 'You will come back for me, though?'

'Haven't I said so?' Jacey Lomax paused with his hand on the door, and Nonie was quite taken by surprise when she found that she herself was now the object of his momentary attention. 'You slept well, Miss Gotthart?' The grey eyes raked her. 'You still look a little peaky to me.'

Raynor swung his chair around deftly.

'*Did* you sleep well, Nonie – after our little midnight chat?'

Colour rushed to Nonie's cheeks. She was well aware that Jacey Lomax's grey gaze had sharpened perceptibly, and she could have cursed Raynor for that unnecessary revelation.

'Quite well, thanks,' she mumbled confusedly, finding that her voice had gone thick with embarrassment, for again every eye seemed to be fastened upon her as though the quality of her slumber had suddenly become a point of quite universal interest.

'A midnight chat?'

Jacey's controlled voice demanded an explanation, just as she had guessed it would. Raynor must have guessed as much, too. Was he doing this deliberately? He certainly seemed to be enjoying the situation, at any rate.

'That's right. Or after midnight, actually, to be precise. What time would you say our tête-à-tête took place, Nonie? One o'clock? No, later, I believe. I distinctly recall the hall clock striking two, don't you?' He chuckled as he studied his brother's changing expression. 'Now, don't come over the heavy brother, Jacey, for God's sake. It was all quite proper, I can assure you. We were simply getting to know each other a little better, that's all, and it was as delightful a process as was possible in my present condition, so you can stop scowling in that arrogant manner. You know damn fine I'm quite incapable of getting up to any mischief at the moment, even if I wanted to. In any case –' he grinned that sudden, devil-may-care grin that could so quickly transform his pain-lined features to a roguish boyishness – 'she looked about ten years old standing there on the verandah in those stripy pyjamas and little bare toes. One can't go around seducing ten-year-olds, can one?'

'What a cosy picture you paint, though, Ray!' Delphine put in creamily. 'And how quickly your little innocent seems to have made herself at home, Jacey, don't you think?'

'It would certainly appear so.' For all his deep tones were so clipped, Jacey Lomax's tanned face was still unreadable as he nodded to the company at large, held open the gauze door for his companion to pass through, and followed her down the steps without a backward glance.

A few seconds later the engine of his car whirred to life, and it slid away smoothly towards the main road leaving a trail of dust in its wake.

'That was unkind of you, Raynor.' Ilse's voice was quietly reproving as she began to gather up the cups. 'Not very nice of Delphine, either.'

'I hope you don't think – they – you don't think—?'

'I don't think anything, Nonie.' Ilse's eyes were sympathetic as they dwelt on the other's distressed face. 'And you mustn't let yourself become upset by Raynor's childish behaviour. He's got a chip on his shoulder as big as that cedar-tree out there. It amuses him sometimes to be cruel, that's all, and I must say Delphine eggs him on. You'll soon get used to it, like the rest of us have had to.'

'No one's asking you to put up with me, Ilse, if that's what you're getting at,' said Raynor hardily. 'Why don't you just go? Go away and leave me, if I'm as difficult as all that. It might be better if you did, at that, for all the progress I'm making,' he tacked on with gloomy cynicism.

'Now, darling, you mustn't say that.' Ilse spoke soothingly, immediately contrite. 'Of course you're making progress. I'm aware of a difference, an improvement, after each session – and I'm speaking now from a purely professional angle. It's there, Ray darling, truly it is. All you've got to do is to believe in it, for it to happen, and it will.' She put her hands on his shoulders, and leaned forward and placed the gentlest of kisses on Raynor Lomax's scowling forehead.

'It's not as simple as that, and you know it,' grumbled Raynor, still frowning, though obviously somewhat mollified. 'You don't just get a thing in life because you *believe* in it. You, of all people, ought to know that by now, Ilse. Sometimes these naïve philosophies of yours simply leave me breathless.'

'One has to believe,' she maintained firmly. 'And it's almost a medical fact of life, Ray, where recovery's concerned. The will has to be there.'

'And you don't think it is, with me?' His tone was bitter. 'Hell, what do you know about it, anyway? Do you honestly think I *like* being here, half man, half wheelchair, dependent upon you, on Jacey, watching you all doing the things I can't do – riding, driving cars, playing tennis, even simple walking? Just walking. The simplest of the lot, and I can't even do that.'

'But you will, Raynor, truly you will. In fact—' she shot a quick look at the neat black watch strapped to her wrist, made an apologetic face – 'I'm sorry, but it's time for another session right now. Goodness knows where the morning has gone to!'

'Let me take these things out and deal with them,' begged Nonie swiftly. 'I know where my own morning has gone, alas – most of it simply in sleeping, so I might as well be useful for what's left of it, don't you think?'

'Bless you, then, if you will. And thanks. After that you might like to look for Pru. She went exploring down through the old orchard, I think.'

'There must be other things I can do first. I didn't come here for a holiday, Ilse, although Mr. Lomax might be forgiven for thinking so when I put in such a late appearance. It was just – well, I felt really terribly tired last night. Tired and sort of confused and apprehensive.'

'You don't need to explain. Of course you'd feel strange on your very first night, but you'll soon get used to us all and learn to find your way around. The orchard is out that way.' Ilse nodded in its general direction. 'Go left outside the kitchen and you can't miss it. O.K.?'

'O.K. And thank you, Ilse.'

'Don't thank me. It was Jacey who arranged it, after all, but I'm going to love having you here. We all are.

Little Pru and Raynor are buddies already, and she's loving being here too. She was so excited about everything this morning, and so interested. She's the adaptable sort, it seems, but then children generally are,' pronounced Ilse tolerantly, as she followed Raynor's wheelchair inside, leaving Nonie to her self-appointed task of clearing away the morning-tea things.

In the kitchen Hattie had returned from the clothesline and was busy scoring cucumber with a fork. Nonie washed and dried the few cups and saucers, and then offered her assistance in other directions.

'Chop those chives, then, if you like.' Hattie's nimble fingers were arranging her cucumber slices around the edge of a large oval platter filled with salad. 'I'll sprinkle it over the lot when you've done it. The board is just behind you – that wooden one there, and here's a good sharp knife.'

'Have you been here long, Hattie? At Tuckarimba? I suppose you have.'

'Not always, if that's what you mean by "long". I came down here when Jacey asked me to. I lived on one of the company's cattle stations when I was up north. My father used to be an overseer with old Mr. Lomax.'

'With the father? And you came down after Mr. – er – Raynor's accident?'

'Heavens, no, long before that. I was here with Jacey when he came here first. I came down to look after him. It's difficult to refuse Jacey a favour when he asks for one.' A pause. 'I must say it's funny hearing you calling him Mr. Lomax. Absolutely *everyone* calls him Jacey.'

'We're not on Christian name terms, exactly.' Nonie swallowed, a little uncomfortably. 'Do you mean here in this house, Hattie? Did Jacey Lomax actually live here, then?'

Hattie scooped up a palmful of chives and sprinkled them deftly over her salad arrangement, stepped back to survey the finished dish.

'That'll do, thank you, Nonie. There's nothing nicer than fresh, crisp salads in this wilting heat, don't you think, and that loam in the garden grows the loveliest lettuces. Lovely everything, come to that. Everything we use here is home-grown,' she added proudly, lifting the platter over to the fridge and placing it on one of the wire racks inside. 'That's more than we could claim up in the top end. We couldn't even have a house-cow up there. Tinned milk, it was, and tinned everything else, almost, except for the sides of salt beef.'

'Did he live here long?'

'Who?' asked Hattie vaguely, her mind already busy with other matters.

'Mr. Lomax – Jacey. You said he lived in this house.'

'For a while, he did, yes.'

'Didn't he like it here? I suppose he couldn't have, or he wouldn't have wanted to sell it.'

'Hmm, I've a feeling the move wasn't Jacey's idea alone. Delphine Simpson took a great interest in the plans for his big new house up there on the hillside, you know, so maybe it was as much her idea as his to part with this one. Who knows? Certainly she never liked it.' Hattie sniffed. 'Not nearly grand enough for the likes of her, I suspect.'

'Nor for him either, I shouldn't think,' murmured Nonie, remembering Jacey Lomax's disparaging, un-sentimental look at the decaying boards and peeling paint before he had taken his leave of her yesterday. It hurt, somehow, that rejection of the old house by them all. It was like a – a personal rebuff, although it was silly to think of it that way, when they couldn't even know that she had ever been remotely connected with it, and es-pecially as she herself now realized what a mistake it had been to come back like this. If Bundy hadn't told her the things that they had been surmising about her father's death, she might have felt differently, but now that she had had that inkling of how things really were, the pain and uncertainty of it all were just another small and agonizing burden, along with the unsatisfactory way Pru had been behaving lately. And her own consequent lack of confidence in herself and her own decisions made everything that much harder to bear, particularly as there was no one in whom she could confide. She was stuck with her own rash decision now, whether she liked it or not.

'Are they engaged, or something?' Nonie dragged her mind back to present realities. 'When she takes such an interest, I mean.'

Hattie snorted.

' "Or something" might be near the mark. There's nothing official, that's what I'm saying by that. Not that Miss Delphine Simpson wouldn't *like* there to be, mind you. She works hard enough at it, heaven knows.'

'You don't like her?' Nonie studied the housekeeper's indignant face, curiously, because she realized with some surprise that there had been a certain genuine vehemence about the way in which the older woman had just spoken.

Hattie drew herself up to her full, not very impressive height, and said,

'It's not my place to like or dislike friends of Jacey's, is it? All the same, I can say I'm surprised at someone like him, someone who's known more women in his day than I'd care to count, falling for that barley-sugar line of hers. That's if he *does* fall for it. Like I've always said, you never really know with Jacey. You never really know what he's thinking and what he's not. He always liked to keep people guessing, ever since I've known him. He's a deep one, Jacey. He's never been the transparent sort, not like *her*. It's not hard to guess what *she's* after. You'd probably spotted it yourself already.'

'She's – well, very attractive,' Nonie pointed out, albeit with reluctance, because she hadn't been able to like Delphine's manner out there on the verandah just now. She hadn't liked that silky sarcasm in her voice, nor the meaning way her eyes had slid from Jacey to Raynor and back to Jacey. And she hadn't much cared for the proprietorial way in which Delphine had rested her manicured hand in the crook of Jacey Lomax's brown forearm as they'd walked down the path to the car.

'Huh, you wouldn't say she was so attractive if you'd heard her sending your little sister about her business the moment she arrived.'

'*Did* she? Did she really do that? I hope Pru wasn't being a nuisance?' Nonie looked suddenly anxious. 'She can be, you know. Where is she now, I wonder?'

'Jacey took her up to show her the kittens under the woolshed. She was quite happy to stay there playing with them. And if I know children the way I think I do, that's what she'll still be doing.'

Nonie found herself unaccountably touched by that gesture of Jacey's. It had been kind of him, to intervene like that, and to rescue Pru from Delphine Simpson's scathing tongue. But then he always seemed to be rescuing someone from something, didn't he? He enjoyed having lame ducks around, just so he could rescue them, it seemed. It was the *way* he rescued you that Nonie didn't like. That high-handed manner, and the way he just *took charge*. When Jacey Lomax took charge, no one else stood much of a chance of doing things in any way but his way, that's what really annoyed her most of all about the man. She'd been doing things her way for years – hadn't had much option, really, since there'd been nobody else to ask in any case – and she meant to go right on doing them her way. Independence was a precious thing, even if you did sometimes make decisions that were stupid and ill-conceived, like the one she had made to come here. Nonie meant to keep her independence, no matter how the Lomax man reacted.

Still, it might have been easier to resist his interference if he wasn't quite so – well – *nice* about it. It might have been easier if he hadn't been so kind, all along, to Pru, either. And it would certainly be easier for Nonie to decide what she should do about the situation she'd got herself into if only little Pru hadn't been going about looking *quite* so happy, *quite* so childishly enthusiastic, over positively everything at Tuckarimba.

Why, even the look on her face this very minute, as she peered out from the semi-dark of the sloping space between the woolshed's slatted floors and the ground where she squatted, to where Nonie herself knelt cautiously beside clumps of docks and nettles calling to her softly – even *that* look told Nonie that Pru was happier than she had ever been in the whole of her not-very-long life.

'Oh, Nonie! Look at them, Nonie, aren't they the sweetest things you ever saw? Come here, sweetness. You darling, come on, then. Look, Nonie, this one's settled on my lap. I think it must like me.'

'The feeling appears to be mutual. You can't go on calling it "*it*" though, Pru. You'll have to think up a name.'

'Yes, that's what Jacey said, and I've named them all already, it's just that I forgot to say them.' Pru grappled with the wriggling bodies, held them up in turn to introduce them. 'I've called the mother Marmalade, like that ginger pussy we had once in Manly. And this is Manda, and this is Reen. Manda*rine*, see. Marmalade, Manda*rine*. See?'

'I see,' nodded Nonie a little faintly, overcome by this stroke of original inspiration, as Pru obviously regarded it. 'Did you tell Jacey what they're to be called?'

'Not yet. He left me while I was still thinking about it. He had to get back to Delphine, I s'pose.' A pause. 'I hate that woman, Nonie.'

'Hate's a strong word, pet.' Nonie did her best to infuse a measure of rebuke into that, but even to her own ears it sounded a bit lukewarm.

'Well, I *do*. She's always so – so smug, so – uppity. First she asked me what I was doing there, and why wasn't I at school, and when I said I wasn't starting till Monday, and Jacey was going to teach me to ride a pony so I can go on that, she said didn't I think I'd missed enough schooling without hanging about with the grown-ups all the time as well. And then she said, Run *on*, child – quite narky sort of. So I did – run on, I mean. Only I didn't really know where to run on *to*, and I was standing at the top of the orchard, where I've got that hopscotch place drawn out, and that's when Jacey came out and told me he had something to show me. Wasn't that nice of him, Nonie? I like Jacey, don't you? I love *him*, and I hate *her*,' Pru added darkly.

Nonie swallowed, amazed at the clarity with which Pru had defined her feelings on the subject. It wasn't going to help things, if besides falling for Tuckarimba, her small sister were to fall for Jacey Lomax as well!

'Don't get too dirty, will you? It doesn't smell all that nice under there, if you don't mind me saying so. You'll need a really good bath when you come back to the house.'

'I know. Jacey said I'll have to, so I s'pose I will,' agreed Pru with some resignation. 'He said it was a condition, or I think that was the word, something like that, anyway. He said they're only here while they're little, though, for protection, see. When they're a bit bigger, they'll come down around the homestead, and Hattie and me'll probably give them scraps.'

'Hattie and I,' corrected Nonie automatically.

'No, Hattie and *me*, because *I'm* in charge of them.'

'Have it your way, poppet.' Nonie grinned at her

sister's indignant retort. 'Only I'm talking about grammar, and you're talking about who'll feed the kittens, and we seem to have got our wires crossed somewhere along the way. I dare say it'll take the schoolteacher to sort that one out.'

'Mrs. Mooney, her name is. Jacey said she's really nice, and she's got kids of her own, too, and they're in the class along with the rest of us. It must be awfully funny having your mother as your schoolteacher as well, mustn't it? But like I was saying to Jacey, I can't imagine what it'd be like having a mother at *all,* even if she was just an ordinary one and not a schoolteacher.'

Here was dangerous ground indeed.

'What else were you and Jacey saying?' Nonie heard herself asking carefully, wondering if perhaps she herself hadn't come into their discussions at some stage, around this point. Surely, though, he wouldn't criticize Nonie and her failings as a guardian to Pru, no matter how incompetent he thought she was? Not to her very own sister?

She was obviously not to be enlightened. All Pru would say (offhandedly. and with her voice muffled because she had buried her face into one of the kittens' furry bodies) was, 'Oh, this and that, Nonie. I can't remember it all, because me and Jacey talk about heaps of things. We tell each other *lots* of things, I mean, don't we?'

'Do you, darling?' replied Nonie with some misgiving, wondering why she should feel so troubled and uncomfortable over the fact that Pru should share so many confidences with Jacey Lomax in this way. They'd only be childish observations and innocent secrets, anyway, probably, like the names for the kittens and things. Harmless chatter, nothing more.

No, she was sure it was nothing more, for in the weeks that followed she took the trouble to observe them together in order to satisfy herself upon this point.

Watching them together as Jacey gave the child her riding lessons, listening to his patient instructions, his quiet teasing when he was with the little girl, and the way in which he listened so attentively to all she had to tell him, Nonie was bound to admit that over this, at least, she might have misjudged Jacey Lomax. He would never use the child to further his own ends or to seek out information, and Pru's chatter itself was harmless enough.

Actually, one couldn't help seeing that Jacey appeared to genuinely enjoy Pru's company, and his censure he reserved for her elder sister. As always, he was – by his own stern code at least – completely just. The younger sister had not yet attained the age of responsibility. The elder one had, and must therefore carry the burden for the joint conduct of their lives, and up to this point it seemed he hadn't much approved of the way Nonie had done things. Not that he wasn't always gravely polite and consistently courteous. He was, but in the most distant fashion. For Pru he had that sudden smile that could break up his rather hawklike features in an instant into scores of little lines that crinkled a fanning pattern at the sides of his dancing grey eyes and grooved a deep path in his weather-beaten cheeks. For Nonie those very same grey eyes held nothing more than an unwavering and inquiring steadiness, with perhaps, at times, a hint of quiet speculation which made her heart thump somewhat uncomfortably whenever she discerned it.

For the first two weeks Jacey rode with Pru to the school, a couple of miles further along the creek, beyond his own homestead. Each morning, for the first week, he came down to the old place on the big bay horse, the same one he'd been leading through the timber that very first time they'd seen him. There he would supervise the catching and saddling of Pru's small chestnut pony, and then they would ride off together on the bridle track along the creek.

At the start of the second week, he insisted that Pru herself must catch her pony and saddle up, and he would join her at a point below his house. By the third week, she was deemed fit to do the whole thing for herself, and make the journey alone.

'There's very little risk,' he took the trouble to assure a concerned Nonie. 'I wouldn't have let her do it if I'd thought there was, but out here in the bush children have to learn to stand on their own feet.'

'And not just children either,' chimed in Delphine sweetly from the doorway. 'I've brought Ilse some more of that tapestry wool she was wanting, since she didn't think she'd have enough to finish the background.'

'She's in the kitchen with Hattie, I think.'

'Is she? I'm in no hurry, anyway.' And to prove her point Delphine took an apple from the bowl on the table and sank down gracefully on one of the cane loungers. 'What are we talking about, anyway, Jacey? Is someone not standing on her own little feet like she should be doing?' She shot a sidelong glance at Nonie.

Jacey's broad shoulders shrugged idly.

'No, Delphine, everyone's doing fine, as it happens. But this is the first day Pru's tackled the ride to school entirely alone, and I'm just reassuring her big sister that she'll be O.K. I've actually arranged with her teacher that if she isn't there by nine o'clock any day that she must phone us, and we in turn will ring her if for any reason Pru isn't coming.'

'Well, that sounds a watertight enough arrangement, and you've devoted quite enough of your precious time to that child in the last few weeks anyway, if you ask me, Jacey.'

'*Did* I ask you, Delphine?' he murmured mildly, raising a bushy brow in mock surprise, and giving a tantalizing grin that took away any suggestion of a sting from his query.

He was rewarded by one of Delphine's most charming and conciliatory of smiles.

'No, you didn't, darling, and I've no intention of interfering. What could possibly happen to the child, anyway, just between here and there?'

Nonie intervened, still hesitant about the whole thing.

'I just thought, if the pony stumbled and threw her off – *you* know—' she gestured a little vaguely – 'And then there's the river.'

'The river?' Delphine's lips curled scornfully. 'For heaven's sake, it's hardly more than a creek, even at its widest, you silly thing. And she can swim, can't she? Even if she couldn't, you could hardly drown a cat in it, it's so shallow. The only person I've ever heard of coming to grief in it was that stupid fellow, the one who was here before your Tintoola lot, Jacey. What was his name, Dermot something-or-other? Only his wasn't an accident. He *meant* to do it, because he was a bit of a flop or something, so everyone said. Lord, you'd *need* to mean to do it, to get drowned in that pathetic little bit of water.' Delphine bit into her apple. 'I dare say even *he* had trouble in actually managing it,' she mumbled less distinctly, adding, as she caught the almost inaudible sigh of Nonie's indrawn breath, 'My dear girl, what on earth are you looking at me like *that* for?'

Nonie found that her hands were clenched against the edge of the table, the knuckles so white that already her fingers felt numb. A dew had broken out on her forehead, and she was wondering a little crazily if, when she unbuckled her fingers from the edge of that table, she might not fall over altogether. She'd have to try it, though. She'd have to get out of here. Outside. Into the air.

Carefully she forced her hands to open.

'It's all right, Delphine.' Could that breathless, faraway gasp really be her own voice? 'I know you – meant to be –

kind – reassuring–' Somehow her wooden limbs moved mechanically towards the door. 'Excuse me – just for a moment–'

Nonie never remembered, afterwards, how she actually got down to the creek, or why indeed she went that way at all. She could only recollect that each dragging step was an incredible effort, as if each foot carried a leaden weight, and that she had to force her limbs into some sort of determined movement. Their direction, their destination, were immaterial.

The trees blocked out the sunshine, the branches mingling, forming dizzy patterns about and above her. Finally she could go no further, but sank down in the grass at the edge of an arc of shingle, lapped by peaceful shallows. There were water-lilies in the pool beyond, their cups closed secretly in the dappled shade that dimpled the broad flat leaves lying so delicately upon the surface of the water. They were serenely lovely, tranquil, calming, of palest cream colour flushed with a mere tinge of pink at the centre.

A sound above her made her raise her eyes. Jacey Lomax stood at the top of the bank. He was hatless, which meant that he had left the house in something of a hurry. Jacey Lomax was *never* separated from that disreputable, wide-brimmed felt hat of his. It was as much a part of him as the springing dark hair, the craggy sun-bleached brows, the cool grey eyes, the firm mouth which just now was pulled into a thin, level line as he picked his way down the bank to where she sat.

Jacey hitched his moleskins and sat down beside her, and Nonie, numb and still as any statue, made a valiant effort to drag her mind out of its trancelike state. She'd need all her wits to cope with Jason Lomax right now, wouldn't she? God, what had she done, fleeing from the room like that?

Nonie drew up her knees and clasped her hands tightly

about them, bracing herself to hide the trembling that still possessed her.

For a time Jacey said nothing, just kept picking up pebbles from the shingle and flicking them into the water with savage little flicks. He selected each pebble carefully, as if it really mattered.

'You seemed upset, Nonie,' he observed at length, still not looking her way, and her heart gave an odd little leap of sheer surprise, not only at his noncommittal tone, but because that was the first time he had ever called her by her name.

She swallowed. Out of sheer nervousness her own fumbling fingers found a pebble, and she too threw it towards the pool. Nonie's pebble didn't reach the water. It landed with a tiny staccato click on the shingle at the edge of the creek.

'I'm sorry,' she said tonelessly. 'I'm quite all right now. It was just a – a – temporary thing.'

'Temporary? Huh!' Jacey gave a snort of disbelief. 'How long have you carried this thing with you without telling anyone?'

'What things?' Her nerves tautened immediately.

Jacey threw away his last pebble without even bothering to see where it went, in a gesture of pure impatience. She knew that he was looking at her now, studying her profile with analytical keenness. Doubtless she was a sight to behold, she realized wryly. She could feel the perspiration setting coldly on her forehead, and her hair clung in pale, sticky tendrils to her temples and nape. A good thing she hadn't actually fainted back there, or she'd be even paler than she probably was.

Jacey continued to study her thoughtfully. He seemed to be waiting. Waiting for *something*, only Nonie didn't know what the something might be. He seemed to be expectant, yet she had no idea what could possibly be expected of her in such a situation as this. It was uncomfortable, sitting there on the bank beside the quiet, expectant, *waiting* figure of Jacey Lomax.

Her nerves began to tingle. Nonie felt her spirit surging back, roused by the man's candid scrutiny. Maybe she could bluff the thing out, if she were clever enough, even though she wasn't feeling particularly clever just now.

'*What* thing?' she repeated, much more firmly.

Jacey's gesture was a peculiarly stern, telling sort of one. And the thing it told her was that her bluff wasn't going to receive the consideration she had hoped it might merit.

'You're Dermot's daughter, aren't you.'

It was a statement, not a question at all. And Jacey Lomax had stated it with such certainty that it was obviously useless to deny it. Too late to bluff, Nonie. Much too late.

The fact that he knew her identity was like a physical blow. She could feel the thud of it as it struck at the pit of her stomach.

'Don't play with me, please, Nonie. I'm hardly in a mood for games.' Jacey's hands bit into her shoulders, turning her towards him. 'Look at me,' he commanded, and when Nonie looked, she saw that indeed he was not in a mood for games.

She swallowed again, and this time she actually heard the difficult sound of it in her throat.

'Yes, I'm Dermot's daughter.' She threw back her head, made herself meet his gaze unflinchingly. There was a defiant note in her voice as she gathered the shreds of her courage about her, and added, 'What if I am?'

Jacey's eyes were unreadable, holding hers. She couldn't look into them for long, especially as he didn't seem to be going to reply.

'H-how long have you – known?' she asked bleakly, glancing away and pushing her hair back nervously. The numbness was draining out of her now, and the old misery was flooding back to take its place again.

'Since the first day you came here to be with Raynor and Ilse,' he told her levelly. 'You never got farther than the wattle tree that evening you came out with Pru to see if the place was for sale. I'd been watching you from the edge of the timber when you were looking for that sign-board, and you didn't go *around* the house that time, you were only at the side where the wattle is. When I brought you here myself you knew your way around too well not to have been here before. The bedroom by the tankstand, you said. Yet you couldn't have seen a tank-stand that night. Even had it been light enough, it's on the opposite side of the house.' His fingers had tightened, bruising the soft flesh beneath her shirt. 'And then there was your reaction inside, that day. Something shook you up pretty thoroughly, even though you tried to hide it, and I asked myself, what?' Jacey released her, shrugged. 'It didn't take much to come up with some answers, and when I checked them out the whole thing dropped into place. Why did you lie to me, Nonie?'

It was her turn to shrug.

'Would you have asked me to come here with Pru if you had known who I was?'

'No, probably not. That's hardly relevant at the moment, though, is it? You lied to me. You deceived me. Why?'

Jacey's face was set, and although his tone was con-trolled, it was full of censure. So full of censure, in fact, that something inside Nonie seemed to snap. This was the old Jacey back – Jacey the god, Jacey the judge, Jacey the arrogant.

'Lie? Deceive?' She scrambled to her feet as she jerked out the words, and he in one swift movement followed suit. 'Who are you to talk of lies, of deceit?' she asked on a rapidly rising note. 'I deceived, yes, because I wanted to redeem my father's name. I wanted to make good, show that I could stick it out, prove I had the guts that you all seem to think Dermot lacked. I was going to paint up the house, and start a market garden, and when I'd got it going, *then* I'd have told everyone, *then* I'd have said, Look, I'm Dermot's daughter, and it wasn't like you all think, because none of you knew him, not like he really was. He was a wonderful father, and I'm proud of him, do you hear, *proud*, not because of what he did, but because he tried. He was weak, but he *tried*. He was human, but he *tried*. We can't all be strong like the great Jacey Lomax, can we? But I'm – I was – going to t-try to be what my father couldn't be, and *then* I'd have told.' The words were pouring out, and Nonie couldn't stop them. Not even when Jacey got her by the shoulders again and shook her could she stop. 'My deceit was justifiable,' she told him shrilly, 'but yours? Ugh! How low, how deceitful haven't you been to me, knowing all the time, and stringing me along—'

'Stop it, Nonie!'

'I won't stop it, I won't! You *have* been stringing me along. Did it give you satisfaction, Jacey? Did you have fun? Knowing all the time, watching me playing out my pathetic little pantomime for your edification and entertainment, enjoying it all from the sidelines while I carried on with my poor little charade like the ignorant clown that I was?' Her voice broke.

'Stop it, Nonie. I'm warning you – stop it!' His tone was low, incredibly deep.

Nonie rallied, unaware of the dangers in that lowness and depth of Jacey's voice.

'I won't, and you can't make me. I don't have to dance to your tune like all the others do. I may be Dermot's daughter, but I'm free to say what I want, and I'm saying it now. You've had your fun, laughing at me behind my back. Well, it's my turn now to say what I think. I hate you, Jacey Lomax, do you hear? I hate you! I—'

Nonie's tirade was halted by Jacey's lips.

They came down upon hers with a savagery of which she hadn't dreamed him capable. At the same time, she was caught against him in such an abrupt and vicelike grip that she was unable to move, let alone struggle. Her head was being forced back, and back, and back. She wondered, dazedly, that her spine hadn't already snapped in two. And still that brutal pressure of Jacey's mouth went on and on, seeking out the rebellion in her, draining the hot protests that rose to her lips with his own lips, so that she couldn't speak, could hardly even breathe.

There was no tenderness there. It wasn't a tender kiss, the way Nonie had always imagined that kisses between a man and a woman must be tender. *Should* be tender. Not tender. Just cruel, and punishing, and – endless.

When he finally released her, Nonie found that she was actually clinging to Jacey's shirt for support. It was a khaki shirt, one of his everyday, bushmen's ones, with shoulder tabs and buttoned flaps on its breast pockets. Nonie had quite a fistful of the khaki cloth clenched in each of her hands, and she had to make sure that she could stand there unaided before she could let go of the shirt at all.

She drew away cautiously, half stupid with shock and fright, aware that she was shaking in every limb. When she put the back of her hand up to her bruised mouth and looked up, finally, at Jacey, he was still looking down at her. It seemed to Nonie that he looked from a great height. His eyes were dark, unfathomable, certainly not repentant.

'Why did you do that?' she asked, cursing her husky, quivering voice.

'Why do you think?' His own tone was uncompromising.

'To p-punish me, I suppose. For the th-things I said?'

Jacey Lomax passed a lean brown hand over his face in a gesture that was curiously weary. Defeated, almost.

'Leave it, Nonie,' he said gruffly. 'You're just a child.'

'No, not that. Anything but that. I haven't been a child for a long, long time. Not since the day my mother died, just after Pru was born.'

There was silence between them for a time. Then:

'Where did Gotthart come in? Was he really Pru's father, or did you adopt the name?'

'No, my mother married him after we left here – down in Sydney. Pru was his baby.'

'I see. That's why there's no mention of him in the local registrar's records. And he actually adopted you, legally?'

'Yes. I took his name. Pru doesn't know that I ever had another name, or a different father. When my mother died, Stroud insisted upon it, because he said it would bind us all close together. He died, quite suddenly, not long after that. I often wondered, as the years went by, whether I should tell Pru or not. I didn't know what to do for the best, and there wasn't anyone I could ask, so I – I – well, I just sort of let things go on as they were. Maybe it was cowardly, but I didn't know what would be best.'

A muscle flickered in Jacey's swarthy cheek. His expression was unreadable, but the bite seemed to have gone out of his voice.

Nonie laughed. It was a nervous, embarrassed little sound.

'Well, Jacey, what do we do now? I mean, where do we go from here?' She gestured uncertainly.

'It's up to you, Nonie. Does it make so much difference to things, the fact that I know, have known for some time about you? I think not. I hope you'll stay as you promised, to help Ray and Ilse? Pru's happy here too,' he reminded her levelly.

'Yes, and *that*'s going to make it harder when we go. Oh, Jacey, I seem to have made such a mess of things, such a miserable mess, and I didn't mean to. Of course I'll stay for as long as I can be of help to Ilse and Raynor, though,' she assured him hastily, stepping back nervously as he moved towards her, 'a – a promise is a promise.'

'That's right, Nonie.' Jacey had come right up to her, but this time all he did, to her intense relief, was to take one of her hands in both of his. He held it there for a moment, captured in a gentle prison of warmth and re-assurance that calmed the rapid flutterings of her re-newed alarm. He turned her palm over, studied it carefully. He seemed to be searching for the right words for what he wanted to say. 'You mustn't worry, Nonie. I only want you to make me another promise, though. It's nothing to do with the other one.'

'What is it? I mightn't be able to.'

'Give it a fair go here, and put the past behind you. In time the pain will go, and you'll feel differently about things. They'll sort themselves out, they always do. None of us has the right to judge another person, only our-selves, so don't let the past get in the way of the present. Pru doesn't know, and you were right not to tell her, *quite* right. No one knows but you, and I.'

'Not even Delphine?'

'Certainly not Delphine. Just you and I,' he emphasized calmly. 'It's up to you whether you ever want to tell anyone or not. I shan't.'

'Thank you, Jacey.'

'And if I can help—'

'No, thanks, you can't,' she was quick to assure him. 'As you said, I'll get over it in time. I don't need anyone's help to do that. It's up to me, isn't it, and I'm sure it'll work out, as you say. I'm sorry I was so silly this morning, rushing out of the room like that. It's just that it was so – so unexpected – Delphine's remark, I mean, and I wasn't ready, I suppose. I wasn't running away, you know.'

The weariness she was feeling couldn't help sounding in her manner, somehow, although she did her best not to let it show. How tired she felt! How dreadfully tired! She wished that she felt stronger to face the thing squarely. Strong, like Jacey Lomax was. Instead, she felt beaten, like someone with a gigantic hangover, except that you could sleep that off, and her problems couldn't be so easily disposed of as that.

'I know you weren't running away,' he replied quietly. 'I don't believe that Dermot's daughter *would* run away, Nonie.'

And, looking into his eyes, and seeing that he really meant what he was saying, Nonie found that she couldn't even answer. Swiftly she turned away and hurried back towards the house, leaving Jacey alone at the edge of the creek.

CHAPTER SIX

'CAN you give them some milk and the bacon and toast scraps from breakfast for me, Nonie? Not till about midday, though.'

That was Pru, her satchel on her back and her lunch-packet already in her saddlebag, squatting down to say a last farewell to the kittens before setting off for school. They were down at the homestead now, as Jacey had predicted, and appeared to have made their home under the tankstand. Only food would lure them out. Although Marmalade, the mother cat, often lay on the concrete outside, sunning herself or washing herself or simply walking up and down purring noisily, all that could be seen of her offspring were two sets of luminous eyes in the darkness beneath the stand.

It was maddening to Pru, who was too big to crawl underneath to play with them.

'One step at a time, kiddo,' Jacey had told her, laughing at her impatience. 'Give them a week or two to get used to the place, and then they'll venture out. Remember everything down here is strange to them yet, after the woolshed. Different sounds, different smells, and human activities thrown in. Wouldn't you be a bit alarmed by all that if you were a kitten?'

'I suppose so. Like me and Nonie when we went to the Pink Pelican. We thought we'd never get used to it, only she said we'd just have to, even if it was a pretty strange sort of dump. I expect that's what Marmalade is telling *them*, too, don't you?'

'I reckon that could be so.' Nonie could just catch Jacey's slow, amused drawl through the gauze of the kitchen window. 'Put down some milk each day, Pru, and any little thing you think they'd like that Hattie can spare, and soon they'll come venturing out for it, as they begin to trust you.'

And that was what Pru had been doing, every day since then. At first, Marmalade came out alone, and carried selected morsels back to her babies, but after a couple of weeks they were edging out cautiously themselves, scuttling back to shelter only if they heard anyone approaching.

'Marmalade won't like the bacon, but Manda and Reen will.' Pru was giving some final words of advice as she unhooked Acorn's reins from the fence post nearby, and climbed nimbly into the saddle.

'Why don't you come riding sometimes, too, Nonie, with Jacey and me?'

'No one's ever asked me to, and I don't suppose there's a spare horse.'

' 'Course there are. There are lots of them, they're taken into the yards every morning. They're all much bigger than Acorn, though, so I don't suppose you'd get on very well anyway.'

'I don't know much about it, so I don't suppose I would,' agreed Nonie humbly – but she was remembering, all the same, those far-off days when she herself had been about Pru's age, and had had a fat pony of her very own.

'I could get Jacey to teach you, if you like.'

'Oh, no, you mustn't do that.' Lord, what would the child think of next!

'He would if I asked him.'

'No, I'd rather not, truly. Pru, I wish you'd leave me out of things when Jacey's around, really I do.'

'Why, Nonie? Don't you like him? I don't think you can, much, and he doesn't think so either.'

'What rubbish you talk!' replied Nonie sharply. 'It's not a question of likes or dislikes. I think I'm completely impartial with absolutely everyone in this household, if it comes to that. Certainly I try to be.'

'What's impartial?'

'Well, it means I like them all the same, and treat them all the same. I don't feel anything more for Jacey than for the others – or any less, either, come to that.'

'Jacey says people who've got very hurt about something sometimes forget *how* to feel. I s'pose that's what im – impartial means.'

'Not exactly that.' Nonie felt her colour rising. 'I hope you and Jacey haven't been discussing me, Pru. I've asked you not to, lots of times.'

Pru looked injured.

'There you go again, Nonie. You *don't* like him, do you? He was only being *nice,* anyway, so there. And it was really me we were talking about, mostly. You only came into it 'cos he said you'd be hurt if I played hookey from school again. He said that working so hard at the Pink Pelican and even *being* in a place like that must've hurt, and that me not going to school might make the hurt worse, that's what he was saying. It was *me* we were talking about, and Jacey's made me promise I won't do it again, and I *have* promised, and I won't.'

'I'm sorry, darling.' Nonie reached up contritely and patted Pru's bare brown knee. 'I don't know what's got into me lately, to sound so cross and unreasonable about everything. I truly am sorry if I sounded narky, and I'm very glad you've promised Jacey that. It's kind of him to think about us the way he does. Now, off you go, Pru, or you'll be late, pet. I'll see to the kittens for you.' She waved from the top of the veranda step. ' 'Bye for now, and take care, darling.'

'So long,' returned Pru, in a fair imitation of Jacey's drawl, although the pitch was a good octave higher.

Nonie sighed as she went indoors. How the child worshipped that man, she pondered to herself, as she carried out the milk and scraps to the back yard before lunch, as she had promised. Every day, every week that passed, their relationship seemed to become more matey – unlike Nonie's own.

She could only feel embarrassment in Jacey's presence these days. Remembering the scalding things she had said that time brought swift, uncomfortable colour to her cheeks whenever she thought of it, even when she was alone and there was no one there to see. Jacey had never referred to the incident again, almost as if he divined her unease. She'd have liked to apologize, but couldn't think how. And then, as she remembered that brutal, remorseless kiss, resentment would begin to smart within her afresh.

Drat the man, why should she even think of saying that she was sorry after *that*?

'Hallo there. How's the kitten girl today?' Raynor's chair came into view from around the corner.

Nonie smiled from her seat on the step. 'Hello. That sun's beginning to be almost too hot, isn't it? And if by "kitten girl" you mean Pru, she's at school, as is usual at this time of the day.'

Raynor stopped his chair at her side.

'I didn't mean Pru. I meant you.'

She pulled a face. 'I'm hardly a kitten-girl, Raynor. I'm a – a *woman*.'

Raynor's cynical mouth quirked a little, as if the quaint dignity of that statement somehow amused him.

'To me you're a child.'

'Why does everyone have to say that?' she asked, piqued. 'That's just what Jacey called me too.' She flushed then, remembering.

'He would,' agreed Raynor equably. 'He likes his women mature, or hadn't you noticed?' A pause. 'Like Ilse,' he added slyly, and Nonie looked at him sharply, aware of the sudden barb in his voice. There he went again, with his cutting remarks that were so calculatingly cruel and unfair! Nonie, this time, had no intention of letting him off with it. She felt she knew him well enough now to protest that it was quite unjust to connect Jacey's name with Ilse's like that.

'You know she's got eyes for no one but you, Raynor. Anyone can see that, and if you can't you're more of a fool than I think you are. Besides, it's Jacey and Delphine, isn't it? You're a fool if you can't see *that* when it's right under your nose, too.'

Raynor grinned, unoffended and unrepentant.

'So the little kitten-girl's got claws. You're barking up the wrong tree, though, my dear, if you'll forgive a slight mixture of metaphors. What you really mean to say is, Delphine would *like* it to be Jacey-and-Delphine. She's aware that I'm aware how hard she's working on it, too. But no—' he grimaced, moved irritably in his chair, 'I'm not a fool, my pet, far from it. I know what I'm talking about. I'm older than you, remember. I know more about these things.'

'*How* do you know?' she challenged him.

'I have the evidence of my own eyes, that's how.'

'What evidence? I've never seen any.'

'Because you haven't been in the right place at the right time, that's why.'

Raynor sighed. It was a jaded sound, and when he looked up Nonie could see that he was deadly serious. In fact, the naked misery in Raynor Lomax's candid blue eyes could not be missed, and certainly not by someone as sensitive as Nonie. He really *meant* what he said.

Somewhere, some time, something had given him this sense of gnawing doubt and unhappiness that had nothing to do with his illness. He was nursing it and fostering it and torturing himself with it, quite needlessly, Nonie was sure. Pity for him swamped her.

'Ray, I don't believe it,' she told him gently. 'Whatever

126

makes you say such things?'

'Because I know them to be true.' He couldn't keep the bitterness out of his voice. 'You must have seen the way he kissed Ilse even that day you arrived. Or don't you remember?'

'I remember very well,' replied Nonie with conviction. 'It was a very nice kiss, I thought. A – a sort of gallant, *considerate* kiss.'

(Much more gallant and considerate than the one he'd given *her*, anyway, she thought fleetingly, and felt that wretched, hot colour flow into her cheeks anew.)

'Pshaw!' Raynor made a sound of pure disgust. 'I don't know why I'm talking to you about it at all, Nonie. You're a child, dear, an innocent, whatever you might like to say to the contrary. Why, do you know that just now you're blushing furiously, even *talking* about a kiss? How could you possibly know how to interpret one when you quite evidently lack the experience even to discuss it without selfconsciousness?'

'Is that one kiss all you have to base your supposition on?' Nonie asked quickly, wishing Raynor's eagle gaze would miss a trick or two just for once.

'No, of course it's not. I'm not as ingenuous as that,' he told her drearily. 'Look, Nonie, there was one occasion in particular, and it put me wise to the whole thing – after the accident, when they thought I was still unconscious. I came round, and there they were standing in the window bay, in each other's arms. And that's God's truth I'm telling you.'

'Well?' she prompted after a moment, for Raynor had stopped speaking, and was gazing into space, his features drawn, his expression brooding, almost as if he had forgotten where he was.

He glanced up when she spoke, forced himself to go on.

'I heard, then, what they were saying,' he continued a

little thickly. 'There they were – embracing each other, remember, Nonie – and Jacey was saying, very low, but I distinctly heard each word he was saying – "Look, Ilse", he said, "if he comes round we mustn't tell him, not yet. If he's going to get better at all, you must carry on like you were, as if nothing had happened, do you understand?" And she said, "Oh, Jacey, I don't think I've the courage, to *pretend* like that. Don't you think it best just to tell him? Maybe he'll actually suspect it, anyway?" and my honourable brother – my *honourable* brother, mark you, Nonie – said "No, Ilse. Better to let him get stronger first, although as you say, knowing Raynor, he might drop to it quicker than we think. He's pretty smart at summing up a situation, but it's better not to put it into words at this stage." And then she buried her head against him, and said she wondered how she could possibly carry it off, and he said she'd have to, just for a little while, to please him. And then he kissed her. That's when he kissed her.'

There was silence after Raynor stopped speaking.

Marmalade came out from under the tankstand, mewed softly, picked up a crust of milk-soaked bread from the tin plate which Nonie had put there, and disappeared into the darkness again.

'I still think it's all a mistake, Raynor,' she said finally, stubbornly, *helplessly*. 'It must be. Maybe you were delirious or something. Maybe you dreamed it. Drugs and things can have strange effects. I mean, the way Ilse *looks* at you—'

'Oh, she can pretend all right – quite a convincing act. I reckon Jacey just got me up here so that Ilse would be near him. Sometimes I just long to let her know that I know, but like the fool that I am I love her too much to actually do it. Even a little of her is better than nothing, you see, and as long as I'm tied to this blasted chair I suppose she'll stick to me through pity. That's how low

I've sunk, Nonie, that I'll keep her with me through pity if there's no other way. God, sometimes I wish I'd died in that benighted hospital. I tried, you know. I tried to have no will to live, but all the time Ilse was there, pulling me back from the brink. That's what love can do, Nonie. It's a damn fool sentiment, believe me. It can make a fool of a man quicker than anything else on this earth.'

Raynor scowled, and Nonie remained silent. How could one answer the unanswerable? What, after all, could she say to this tortured and bitter man?

'Jacey knew Ilse before I did, you know, Nonie,' Raynor informed her after a while, inconsequently. 'You *didn't* know that, did you?' He had been quick to spot her unconcealed surprise. 'Oh yes, he did. It was Jacey who met her first. I don't know whether he'd taken her out before that time he brought her back to the house we'd rented at the beach that year – probably he had, although people we'd met on the beach used to drift in and out, too, and there were always plenty of women in Jacey's life. You'd never know what he was thinking, even in those days, or how serious he was about any of them, but I knew, the moment I saw Ilse, how serious *I* was. I went after her from the start – I couldn't help myself. It gradually seemed that we drew closer all the time, and while the others still went in a sort of crowd to things, Ilse and I would find ourselves coupled together. Eventually I asked her to marry me, and she said she would. And then, only about a month after that, I was playing in a polo match – and the rest you know. Oh, damn, damn, *damn!*' Raynor struck the arm of his chair with his open palm in sheer frustration. 'I shouldn't have opened out to you like this, child – I'm sorry, Nonie. There's no need to look so stricken. Forget I ever spoke of it, will you? I wish *I* could.'

He swung the chair around deftly and sent it off at a furious speed, and Nonie, sighing briefly, got up off the step and went inside to help Hattie to prepare the lunch.

Raynor seemed withdrawn, preoccupied for much of the meal, but Ilse, if she noticed, responded with her usual calm tranquillity. Nonie, meanwhile, did her best in the next few weeks to provide cheerful and diverting company for both Ilse and Raynor. That was what she had come here for, so far as Jacey was concerned, and she'd have to live up to her promise.

She couldn't find it in herself to believe the things that his own brother had attributed to Jacey Lomax. He was autocratic, domineering in a way that roused her own spirited resentment, but – underhand? No.

And yet he had been, with her, hadn't he, pretending all this time that he didn't know she was Dermot's daughter when all the time he *had* known it. Nonie found herself wondering how long he'd have let her go on playing out her forlorn little charade if Delphine hadn't surprised her into revealing her identity to him that day. Would he have bided his time, trapped her himself, some day – intentionally? It was all too confusing to know with any certainty just what would have happened. She could only be thankful that Jacey had never referred to the matter again.

Unwillingly, Nonie asked herself if he sometimes remembered that confrontation like she did. If he did, it was probably with the patronizing amusement that a man of his experience might bestow on a mere babe in arms. The memory of it, as always, was infuriating, and filled her with an odd kind of despair. She found it difficult to conceal her awkwardness when Jacey was around, these days, and avoided him whenever she could.

Delphine was about a lot these days too, and speculation was in the air. One could almost feel it, physically, so tangible was it. Nonie and Hattie would often see the small yellow sports car weaving its way up the hill to the other homestead, where doubtless Jacey's own house-keeper would have a meal prepared for them. Nonie could imagine the two of them sitting together on the verandah, looking out over the valley and the winding creek below. She tried not to think along those lines, though. Heaven knew why, except that the mental tableau gave her a feeling of vague unhappiness. Jacey had only taken her up to his new house the one time since she had come, and even then Delphine had been there. She had been quite charming to Nonie that day, as if she were in truth a mere visitor, a bare acquaintance, and Delphine herself the proper mistress of the house. In the subtlest of ways, her manner had indicated that she was in possession, and she even took it upon herself to show Nonie around the place, almost as if it were her own.

Nonie had been somewhat aghast at the sheer luxury of it, the roominess, the size. The kitchen was lavishly appointed, air-conditioned, tiled. The bathrooms and showers had the latest chrome fitments and beautiful terrazzo floors. The verandahs were columned with white pillars in the colonial style, and already colourful creepers that Jacey had had planted were beginning to twine their way up from their bases.

It made the old homestead seem more of a shambles than ever by comparison, although Nonie and Ilse worked hard to restore it to some sort of order.

As Jacey had originally pointed out, what it really needed was a complete, professional renovation, whereas the most that she and Ilse could do was to tidy up the place and scrape off some of the flaking paint, renewing it where they could. They were working their way through the rambling building, gradually, room by room, but their efforts were only moderately successful. Whenever they put on new paint somewhere, all the rest looked relatively worse by comparison. Nonie had a feeling that they were fighting a losing battle, although she never said as much to Ilse. It would have been too disheartening, actually putting her doubts into words – and besides, it gave Ilse something to do when Raynor's moods were upon him, and it was a welcome escape when he was choosing to be particularly difficult.

In contrast to her elder sister, Pru was often up at the new place. Sometimes she called in there on Acorn on her way back from school, and sometimes Jacey took her up himself. There was nothing the little girl liked more than to sit in the back of his Toyota truck with Jacey's two blue cattle-dogs for company beside her and the breeze lifting her short brown hair into elfin spikes as they went along. He took her with him to some of the huts further out, too, putting out salt blocks for the stock to lick, cleaning bore-drains, mending windmills, tightening fences.

It was on her return from one such excursion that Nonie, having lit the old chip-heater and supervised the running of her sister's bath, was confronted with something of a problem – a minor one, but embarrassing, nevertheless.

As she was sorting out the tumbled heap of clothes on the floor, left there by Pru before she stepped into the yellow water, the child's voice came conspiratorially from the bathtub.

'Nonie, I've got a secret.'

'Mm?' Nonie's mind was on other things.

'Well, a sort of secret. You an' me are the only ones that know. And Jacey will, of course,' she added importantly.

That captured her sister's attention all right!

'Jacey?'

'We're going to give him a present.'

Nonie regarded her, nonplussed.

'Darling, we can't do that. We haven't any money – well, not the sort that would buy someone like Jacey Lomax a present, anyway. Whatever put that idea into your head?'

''Cos it's his birthday,' Pru crowed triumphantly from the suds. 'Two weeks today, exactly. Mrs. Parsons told me, and she's going to make him a birthday cake, and I can come up and eat some. She said so.'

'Is he having a party, then?'

'Well, sort of. Mrs. Parsons says we can all come if we like. But it was *my* idea.'

'I see,' Nonie said weakly. 'And what do you suggest we give him, poppet? A yacht for the beach when he goes down to Sydney? Or another aeroplane? Or do you think he'd like a fabulous new bull, one of those prize pedigree ones?'

'Silly!' Pru couldn't restrain a giggle at the grand gestures Nonie was making as she suggested these various possibilities. 'I *know* we haven't got the money for that sort of thing. I *know* we have to save it all up so we can buy this dear old house one day. But this won't take any money at all, hardly even a dollar.'

'What won't?'

Pru put down the sponge she had been wielding and lolled back, a small smirk of satisfaction playing about her lips.

'What I've decided on.'

'And what have you decided on, may I ask?'

'A sign, silly.'

'A sign?'

'A nameplate thing, for the new house. A nice big wooden one. He hasn't got one, and you can do them so beautifully, Nonie. It'll hardly cost a thing, see, because you've still got your brushes and stencils and paints and stuff, haven't you? He'll just *love* it,' Pru said enthusiastically.

'I doubt it.' Nonie gazed at her sister's ecstatic face helplessly. 'I – I don't think I could, Pru. Not for Jacey.'

'Why do you say that?' her sister demanded back,

giving her a curious look. 'Jacey said you wouldn't want to, as well.'

Nonie was startled by this rather breathtaking revelation. 'I thought you said it was a *secret*?' she remarked dubiously.

'So it is. I didn't tell him *what* it's going to be, stupid, only that I was going to get you to make him something for his birthday. Something special, that you're really good at.'

'And what did he say to that?'

'Well, he did look sort of funny and doubtful, now I come to think of it. Then he said he didn't think you might want to, not for him. And he told me to forget about it, and I said I wouldn't forget about it, that I'd ask you anyway. I don't want to forget about it, Nonie. Honestly, I don't. I want to give it to him, because he's given me such a lot of things, like the kittens for my own, and the pony, and – oh, heaps of things. Please say you will, Nonie, please! It's only a little thing, and you've made them for heaps of people, so why not for Jacey? And I've *said* you're going to, so don't be a meanie.'

Nonie didn't want to be a meanie, and it looked as if Pru had taken the thing too far for her to be able possibly to retreat. If she refused, and there was no gift forthcoming, Jacey would know she hadn't wanted to do it. And if she bought him some small, impersonal thing from them both, which she'd much prefer to do, he would realize that she'd been reluctant to make him something herself, and he would be as embarrassed as she was that Pru had sort of compromised them both. Whatever way one considered it, she was cornered.

Oh dear, why did children have to land their elders in such difficult situations as this one?

Pru's hopeful face was still peeping over the towel she had enveloped around herself, and that face looked so scrubbed and innocent that capitulation seemed inevitable.

Nonie sighed.

'O.K., Pru, just this once. But another time,' she warned sternly, 'another time be sure to talk it over with me first.'

She wasn't in any great hurry to do the thing, somehow, but with a week gone already since Pru had first mentioned the project, she at last decided that she had better get going. If she was to do it at all, she might as well do it properly. Anyway, she had to admit that she enjoyed tackling anything creative like this, and as she went to her room and searched out the necessary bits and pieces of materials from her luggage, she found herself actually humming softly.

Four days later she produced her handiwork for Pru's inspection.

'Yes, I *like* it,' the latter murmured admiringly. 'What a lovely piece of wood!'

It was, too – a particularly attractive slab of Jacey's own mulga, off his very own property. Nonie had searched hard before picking out a specimen of suitable shape, and then she'd taken the thing into Tuckarimba township and got one of the builders there to saw it flat across the grain for her. The result was a most unusual, almost kidney-shaped signboard, and she had further highlighted its engaging shape by following the outline with an edging of pokerwork. The name itself – a simple 'Tuckarimba' – was in plain sloping print.

'Nonie, could you just put some gold on around the edges of the letters, do you think, and then some more black? You know how you do, so it looks as if they're all turning sideways? I always love it when you do them that way, it's as if the sun's sort of shining through it, and there are shadows at the back of the words.'

'Well, I suppose I could. I like it plain, myself.'

'I think me and Jacey might like it best turned sideways.'

Nonie had to smile at that.

'O.K., have it your way.' It was Pru's present, after all.

It took her most of the rest of the afternoon to touch it up in the way Pru liked, the gilt edging first, for the thick strokes, and then the finest black outline again.

'How about that?' she asked at length, holding it up once more. 'Careful, Pru. It's not dry yet.'

'I think it's gorgeous, honest I do. And so will Jacey! Nonie, thanks for doing it. You really *are* clever' – and her little sister's sudden, impetuous hug was somehow ample reward for the pains which Nonie had taken over the work.

Jacey's birthday was on a school day, and when Pru had returned in the middle of the afternoon she found that her sister had her parcel already done up for her.

'Can you carry it on Acorn, do you think? I'm sure you can, if I hand it up to you once you've got on.'

'I've unsaddled him, Nonie, and turned him loose. I thought we'd walk up.'

'We?'

'Well, you're coming too, aren't you?'

'I wasn't going to, no.'

'Oh, Nonie, *please*!' Pru's expression of anticipation had abruptly changed to one of plain and shattering disappointment. 'Please. I mean, I've thought you'd come with me all along, and Mrs. Parsons is expecting you. She's promised you a bit of birthday cake when we cut it. It's going to have blue icing and everything.'

'You could bring me back a piece, darling.'

'Nonie, it's not the *same*!' Pru's voice was a wail. 'It won't be half as much fun if you're not there. You know we always share everything, we always have.'

'Very well, then, Pru, if you'll be so disappointed.'

'I will be, Nonie, I will.'

'Very well, then. Wait a second till I go and get tidied a

bit first.'

When they got up to the new homestead a quarter of an hour later, Nonie found herself wishing that she had in fact taken even longer and tidied up a little bit more than she hurriedly had, for the sight of Delphine's yellow car filled her with dismay.

For two pins she'd have turned back, Pru or no Pru, but their approach had already obviously been observed, by one person at least.

'Pru, is that you at last? School must've been late out today, surely? Come on, lasses, we've been waiting for you to show up before I put the tea through.' So saying, Mrs. Parsons bustled off towards the kitchen, around the side of the house, and Nonie smoothed her palms a little nervously down the sides of her jeans and followed across the lawn as her small sister negotiated the front steps carefully, with the brown paper parcel in her hands.

At the top the gauze door was thrown open. Pru put down the parcel unceremoniously and rushed right into Jacey's arms. They'd been held wide inviting her to do just that, and Nonie could see that, as he hugged the child, he wasn't bothering to hide the fact that he was pleased to see her.

'Thanks, scrap,' he grinned in reply to her birthday wishes, adding a little ruefully, 'Not that I'm as keen on marking my advancing years as you appear to be!'

'Many happy returns, Jacey.' Nonie stepped forward awkwardly, put out her hand, aware of Delphine's mocking eyes upon her as she did so.

'Thank you, Nonie.' Gravely he took the extended hand. 'I see you've got involved in this affair too.' A smile crinkled his eyes. 'I'm beginning to wonder whose birthday it really is, your little sister's or mine.'

Jacey pulled up a chair for her. Tea was set out on the table beside Delphine, and Mrs. Parsons must already have brought the pot in, because there it was, too, with a matching silver water-jug, steaming faintly at the spout.

Again Nonie wished she'd smartened up a bit more, Delphine made such a graceful picture presiding over the teapot. Her sleeveless dress of straw-coloured tussore was superbly cut, and its matching jacket Delphine had placed over the back of the chair behind her head, so that her wonderful auburn hair was foiled by the jacket's emerald lining. The combination was entrancing, and one could hardly blame Jacey Lomax for finding it so, as he obviously did. His eyes were resting appreciatively on Delphine's features – the beautifully tanned, absorbed face with its faint dusting of freckles, and those unusual yellow-green eyes.

'Thanks for pouring for us, Delphine. Scones and sandwiches to begin with, young 'un, and *then* I'll cut the cake,' he told Pru, laughing at her expression as she somehow managed to drag her eyes away from the layered confection that Mrs. Parsons had made to mark the occasion, and instead took one of the proffered scones.

Jacey passed Nonie her cup, and only then did she register the fact that he, too, was dressed more formally than usual. No khaki bush-shirt today, but a crisp white one, the sleeves rolled up to reveal his muscular brown forearms, a patterned tie at his throat. His trousers were narrow-cut, creased, evidently part of a tropic-weight suit, for he'd put the jacket over the back of his chair like Delphine had, except that his had been flung there rather more carelessly.

Delphine had seen Nonie's eyes on the jacket.

'Don't feel bad that you haven't dressed for the occasion, my dear,' she said, quite kindly. 'You're quite all right as you are. You see, it's not for *this* occasion that either of us is dressed at all.' She smirked. 'Actually Jacey's taking me for dinner in town tonight to celebrate his birthday. So when Pru wanted this little party first, we decided that we'd get ourselves ready beforehand, and then we wouldn't have to rush things quite so much. She was obviously terribly enthusiastic about there being a proper birthday tea, and we wouldn't have dreamed of disappointing her.'

'Thank you, Delphine,' Nonie replied as gratefully as she could, for inwardly she was grinding her teeth at the smug way in which the other girl could manage to put things across. 'And I'm quite certain she's not a bit disappointed, are you, Pru? It's a really beautiful cake, isn't it? Jacey says you're to take some back for Ilse and Raynor and Hattie afterwards.'

'And you've got to open your present now, Jacey. It's from me and Nonie, and you've got to open it now and see what's inside.'

To Nonie's secret dismay, her young sister had leapt up with determination and was now lugging the ungainly parcel across the floor from the place where they had propped it against the wall after they first came in.

'It doesn't look too breakable, anyway,' Jacey grinned, 'not the way you're treating it. Careful, Pru,' he added sharply, as she gave it a final nudge in his direction with her foot.

'Oh, it won't break, don't worry. You'll see. Nothing can break it, Jacey, except – well, something really *big* could, I s'pose, but usually they last almost for *ever*.'

'For *ever*? That's a pretty long time. Whatever can it be?'

Jacey's fingers were undoing the knots, and he was taking his time. He was doing it just to tease Pru, and as she hovered around his shoulder he turned and winked at her. When he unwound the wrapping and revealed the gift itself his expression changed.

'Nonie made it. I told you she was going to make you something. You see, Jacey, it is special, isn't it? Do you like it?'

Jacey was studying his present with interest. He ran his brown fingers over the smooth surface of the polished mulga, inspecting the lettering and the way in which it was done.

'Yes, it is special, Pru. And yes. I do like it. I like it very much, thank you. Thank you *both*,' he stressed, and just for an instant his eyes caught and held Nonie's.

'It was nothing,' she mumbled awkwardly, acutely aware of Delphine's curiously still figure beside her. 'Nothing. I did it for Prù.'

'Yes, I know.' Jacey's tone was suddenly bland. 'Still, you put a great deal of work into it, and the result is beautiful.' Once again his eyes caught and captured hers, and this time there was some sort of message in them, a message that Nonie quite failed to translate.

'I mean that, Nonie. I shall treasure it.' There was such a sober honesty about the way Jacey added that that she heard herself say quickly, a little huskily,

'*Do* cut your cake, Jacey. Pru is simply dying to have a bit.'

'Yes, do, darling,' Delphine interpolated, gracefully assuming charge of the operation again. 'We'll all have a piece, and then I shall ask Mrs. Parsons to wrap some up, and the girls can take it back to the others. We shall need our time if we're going to look in at the Club first, and I did promise I would, remember?' she reminded him, with just the right amount of hesitant apology in her tones.

After that, there wasn't much to do but eat one's piece of cake and depart with as little delay as possible, was there?

Walking back in the semi-darkness with Pru towards the old homestead at the bottom of the valley, Nonie had to admit to herself that she hadn't enjoyed it much. In fact, the whole afternoon had been a bit of an ordeal from start to finish. The only warming thing had been the sincerity of Jacey's appreciation, his kindness towards them both. That hadn't been in any doubt, and yet probably because it had been directed towards her as well as Pru, Nonie found it intensely embarrassing, although she wouldn't for the world have said so to Pru, who was busy enthusing all the way home. The whole set-up had been made even more uncomfortable by the very presence there of Delphine Simpson. Not that she too hadn't been kind, even gracious, in an offhand sort of way, but at the end Nonie had sensed an alienation between herself and Delphine, a hostility that was almost a physical current passing from one woman to the other, from Delphine over to her. Maybe she had imagined it, but she didn't think so. Yet she could be wrong, because as they'd left, Delphine had waved a languid hand in her direction and said, quite sweetly really,

'Good-bye for now, Nonie. And you must come into town and see me some time, so that we can get to know one another a little better.'

Nonie hadn't known quite what to say to that, if she were to be honest, so she had simply smiled, and returned the wave somewhat unconvincingly. Delphine always made her feel ungroomed, gauche, and incredibly – well, *young*. A child, in fact. A child, like Jacey and indeed Raynor had already defined her to her own face. It was galling to be thought of in that way, when you'd been a fully responsible guardian for years and years and when, at times, you felt about a hundred years old.

Anyway, as it turned out, Delphine was as good as her word about arranging to see her again, and only a few days later she issued an invitation which Nonie would have felt churlish in refusing.

It was Ilse who had taken the telephone call.

'By the way, Nonie, Delphine rang and asked for you, but you were out at the chooks or somewhere, and I couldn't seem to find you. She was in a hurry, so she left a message. She wondered if you'd be kind enough to help her on one of the Country Women's Association stalls at the Sale on Friday. Janet Daniels who was to be on it with her has gone sick, so I said I was sure you would not mind helping out.'

'What would I have to do, Ilse?'

'They're on produce, so it'll be as simple as pie. You'll need to go in early to help to price everything as it comes in, and once the sale's open, it's just a case of selling the stuff and doling out the right change. It will be a nice break for you, and you'll get a chance to meet some of the other country people from the stations farther out. They all come in for it. And you can take my car, Nonie, I told Delphine not to bother to collect you. I'll be here for Pru coming home from school, so there's nothing to worry about at this end.'

They seemed, between them, to have it all arranged.

'O.K.,' she agreed a little faintly. 'I suppose I'd better.'

'Of course you will! It'll do you good. Jacey was only saying the other day that you're still looking a little bit off colour and strained, and I felt quite guilty because I knew how hard I've been working you, with all that painting and scraping that we've been doing.'

'Nonsense, Ilse, I've enjoyed it. We'll clean out the store next week, shall we? I know you've been wanting to go through all that junk that he more or less threw in there out of sight when he came here.'

'Mm, yes. It may be out of sight, out of mind with Jacey, but I can't feel that way, I'm afraid. Whenever I look in the door I nearly have a fit. I'm sure we can at least tidy it up, anyway, if not get rid of quite a lot of it.'

'Ilse, I – I hope I won't meet any of the customers from the Pink Pelican when I'm on the stall,' Nonie ventured shyly. The thought had been worrying her not a little ever since Ilse had brought up the matter. 'I mean, Delphine is so – so fastidious and refined, isn't she, and they were a pretty lewd bunch, you know. I would hate to be the means of embarrassing or offending her.'

Ilse put back her head and laughed.

'My dear Nonie, I can see just what you mean. I'd forgotten your shady and suspect past! But don't worry on that score. It'll be almost exclusively a women's thing, I should think. I doubt if there'll be a man in sight – and certainly not the kind who frequent the Pink Pelican. They'd want something a little stronger than a C.W.A. cuppa and a lemonade, which is about all there'll be.'

Thus reassured, Nonie went off to string some beans for Hattie.

When Friday came she got up early to light the heater and wash her hair. It was almost dry, and becoming fairer every minute as the dampness went out of it, by the time she went to get out Ilse's old blue Chev.

She was reasonably pleased with her navy linen button-through, too. It looked businesslike and yet feminine, and to boost her own confidence while in Delphine's elegant company, Nonie had made up her face with more care than usual, using a soft rose-pink lipstick, and mascara on her abundant lashes.

'Would you like to borrow these? The sun's quite strong.' Ilse, looking her over with approval, handed her her own blue-framed sunglasses. 'Yes, you look good, Nonie. I've never seen you all dressed up before.'

'Neither have I, young 'un, and yes, you do look rather good. Simple but stunning – or should I say "simply stunning"?' Raynor had wheeled himself over to join Ilse in a final inspection. He was in one of his more amiable, faintly bantering moods. 'See and stand at the back of the counter or they might put you up for the raffle.'

'You make me sound like a cellophane-wrapped chicken! Well, I'll see you both later.'

Nonie let in the clutch and reversed away from them with care, waved again, and finally bounced sedately down the track to the main road.

The sale was out at the pavilion at the Showground. When Nonie got there there were already a number of cars parked under the gums near the entrance. They mostly belonged to the stallholders who had come early to arrange their wares, but cars came and went right up to the time of the official opening, and Nonie found that she was kept busy accepting goods, discussing what should be charged for them, and finally labelling them with the little price stickers which Delphine had given her for the purpose. Delphine herself worked surprisingly hard and competently, arranging boxes of tomatoes, eggs, and jars of honey, lining up jams and fruit and pickles, stacking mountains of green speckled water-melons, succulent palest green cucumbers, prickly chokoes, grey-green pumpkins, and attractive little round rock-melons with lacy skins that looked as if they'd been dipped in cobwebs.

'Will we ever manage to dispose of it all?' asked Nonie, surveying the growing pile dubiously.

'You wait and see,' replied Delphine obscurely – and to Nonie's amazement they did. Almost all of it, anyway.

As they were clearing up the debris at the end, there only remained a couple of pumpkins and a longish yellow-striped melon or two.

'Those ones are jam ones, that's why.' Delphine looked up from where she was placing the money into neat little piles prior to making a final count. 'Not everyone can be bothered going to all the fuss involved in melon jam, though. It's quite a palaver, really. Leave them there, Nonie, and I'll take them myself. How much are they marked at? I'll take them out to Mrs. Parsons, and she'll know what to do with them. Jacey's particularly fond of melon jam.' A pause, during which Delphine reached for her handbag and took out a small leather purse. Having placed the price of the melons carefully in the kitty with the rest of the day's takings, she snapped the little purse shut again and put it back inside the larger handbag. 'By the way, Nonie, I feel I must just say a word or two to you about that.'

'About what?' Nonie looked over, somewhat startled by the other's clearly determined manner.

'About Tuckarimba, in general.' Delphine made a small move with her pretty red lips, spread her manicured fingers a little deprecatingly. It's for your own good, my dear, believe me. I hesitate to speak of it, I don't particularly *want* to speak of it, but after the other day, after Jacey's birthday, I realized that I must.'

'Go on.' Nonie was beginning to feel curiously apprehensive. She wished that Delphine would get to the point.

'I think you will have to remember,' Delphine continued with clarity and a definite air of purpose, 'that you are an employee out at Tuckarimba, and it would not be wise for you to try to step outside that role.'

'I – don't understand.'

'My dear Nonie, I think you do. Don't you think, for instance, that it was a little presumptuous of you to make Jacey *quite* such a personal gift for his birthday – or indeed to give him a birthday present at all? It was obvious that you had spent a vast amount of time and thought and attention upon it, wasn't it. I mean, if it were to be something from Pru, a small box of chocolates would have been appropriate. The whole thing was so obviously *your* notion.' Another pause. 'I think you made – shall we put it charitably? – an error of judgment. It was an unwise choice, my dear, too personal, too intimate, and therefore in bad taste. I shall be grateful, if, as an employee, you in future show a little more care and circumspection in your actions. That's all.'

She made a dismissive gesture, and would have returned to her counting, but Nonie, her face aflame, somehow stood her ground.

'Aren't you being a bit presumptuous yourself, Delphine? I don't quite see where *you* come in. What right have you to reproach me like this, over something that can't concern you?'

'But it does concern me, Nonie,' corrected Delphine coldly. 'It concerns me very much, as Jacey's future wife. As the future mistress of Tuckarimba.'

Nonie gaped. She felt dazed, a little breathless, as if she'd been dealt an actual blow.

'You – are you *engaged* to Jacey Lomax?' she insisted hardily, because now she was recalling Raynor's bitter face, his persistent misery, his unhappiness in the fixation he had that Jacey loved Ilse Bjornig.

Her eyes sought Delphine's ringless left hand, and Delphine's own eyes followed them.

'One doesn't rush a man like Jacey Lomax, my dear. He prefers to make the running, and take his own time. I don't need a ring to prove his affection for me, but I'm beginning to think it might be wise to display one, all the same, just to clear up any possible misconceptions. Believe me,' she stressed, taking in Nonie's dubious expression, 'there is a very clear understanding between Jacey and myself. Further than that I am not prepared to elaborate. Why should I, and to *you,* a mere servant – although I'm not too sure that you'll remain one for very long once I'm in charge out there. There can be too many women about the place unless their roles are very clearly defined. It can make for complications, I often think. Just remember your position out there, in the meantime, will you, and the reason Jacey took you on at all.'

Delphine turned back to the piles of notes and change, and Nonie went on clearing up mechanically. When she had carried the last of the remaining cartons to the boot of Delphine's car, she came back again, said tonelessly,

'That's it, then, Delphine. I think I'd better be going back now.'

Delphine glanced up.

'Do you know how much we've cleared? A hundred and eighty-four dollars, sixteen cents. Not a bad day's work, after all. Tell Ilse that figure, will you, and thank her for lending me your services for the afternoon. You were a great help, Nonie.'

Nonie mumbled as gracious a reply as she could muster and took her leave, thankful to at last be able to get away.

How ghastly it had all been, that ticking off of Delphine's! She wanted to nurse her embarrassment to herself, to lick her wounds in private. Although why that particular expression should come to mind right now, it was beyond her to think. What wounds had she to lick, for heaven's sake?

She scrambled into the old blue Chev and rattled off, around the white-railed arc of the racecourse, out on to the Tucka road. Her mind was a jumble of incoherent thoughts and emotions, and she felt sore and bruised and confused.

It was only when she was half-way home, and the soreness exploded into a great tide of pain, that Nonie knew, with clarity, the answer.

She was in love with Jacey Lomax herself.

CHAPTER SEVEN

It didn't help matters much on arriving home to find Jacey there himself. He and Ilse and Raynor were sitting having a drink on the verandah when she came through the gauze door.

'Hello, there,' Raynor called immediately. 'Come and join us. How did things go?' Then, as she came nearer, 'Good lord, what did they do? Run over you with a steamroller? You look all in.'

She managed a pale smile. 'It was a longish day,' she admitted briefly, accepting the drink that Jacey had poured for her. 'I guess I'm not used to that sort of thing – the people and the standing.'

It must have sounded lame. Jacey thought so, anyway.

'I'd say you were more than used to it,' he contradicted, giving her one of those long, shrewd looks. 'You'd plenty of it at the Pink Pelican, under much more strenuous circumstances than a mere women's get-together at a country fête.'

'Maybe so.' Nonie was not prepared to argue. She compressed her lips, and wondered that it showed so much. Certainly she felt different, so maybe she looked it too. So long as nobody guessed the *reason*—

'The wringer, not the steamroller,' she corrected Raynor, grinning gamely and ignoring his brother's nearness as best she could. 'I feel a bit wrung out rather than flattened. The heat was wilting, and the sun was right on our particular stall for the whole afternoon, although some of them were more under the trees and got some shade. Thank you for the glasses, Ilse, they really were a necessity, as you'd guessed.'

'They suited you.' Ilse smiled gently. 'How did the actual sale go?'

Nonie related the day's total.

'We had masses to sell. Rather many preserves and eggs, but we got rid of them all in the end. We had fun, really.'

'Yes, it *looks* as if you'd had fun.' Jacey's voice, deep and sarcastic, sounded in her ear as he leaned over and prized her fingers from the stem of her glass. 'If you hold on to that any tighter it'll crack in two under the strain. Why so tense?'

'Just leave me alone, will you, Jacey?' she snapped, more irritably than she intended. His nearness, her awareness of it, were almost intolerable. She had no idea that discovering oneself to be in love could be such a traumatic business.

His mouth took on an unpleasant twist, the grey eyes narrowed.

'Take a sip of that drink, little one,' he bade her, handing back the glass. 'It might help to sweeten you up a bit.'

'I'm not aware that I need sweetening up, thank you,' she retorted coldly.

'Nonsense. There's a certain acrimony about your approach that wasn't there before. If it's tiredness that's caused it, the sooner you hit the hay tonight the better.' A pause. 'Were there just the two of you on that stall? You and Delphine?'

'That's right.'

'Did she work you too hard?'

'I'm not complaining, am I? She worked darned hard herself too. As I said, it was a successful day. Well, if you'll excuse me—' she put down her drink, almost untouched – 'I think I'll go and – and have a wash and change out of this dress.'

'Take your time, Nonie,' Ilse said kindly. 'We can

149

always have our meal a little later than usual. You'll stay, Jacey, and have a bite with us?'

'Not tonight, thanks, Ilse,' he replied tightly, reaching for his hat and getting to his feet. 'I don't think the vibrations around here are too friendly at the moment, certainly not sufficiently to persuade me that my presence at your table would be unanimously welcomed.'

Nonie, already at the entrance to the hall, couldn't miss the bite in his deep voice, and a quirked brow in her direction left her in no doubt that the remark was aimed at her. She was thankful to escape before he could discern the painful colour that crept into her cheeks, even though there was a certain temptation to stay and answer back. Even now she couldn't take that domineering manner without wanting to fight back. In fact, more than ever now, she'd have to fight back when Jacey tried to dictate, wouldn't she? More than ever now she'd need to assert her independence, steer clear of involvement, emotional or otherwise. It would never do to succumb to his autocratic charm, although, when you loved a man with the steady, constant ache that was beginning to plague Nonie, it would have been the easiest thing in the world to succumb.

She managed, in the next couple of weeks, and by sheer dint of willpower, to adjust to the discovery she had made about herself. The utter hopelessness of it forced her to a sort of compromise, so that she could go about her everyday tasks with a reasonable semblance of normality. It seemed to her that she had been fighting against hopeless situations for most of her life, and therefore it was nothing new to have to do it once more.

Together she and Ilse got down to the last of the scraping and repainting that they'd been doing, and after that they moved on to the store. It was a long, narrow room at the rear of the main wing, lit by a single electric bulb. To increase the light in the corners, Nonie had removed the shade, but even then she found they needed a torch apiece, to play along the dusty shelves and into the cobwebby cupboards, so that they could see exactly what was there.

Never had Nonie come across such a conglomeration. Stacks of old crockery, none of it matching, pots and pans minus handles or lids, saddlery and harness, bolts of calico, piles of grey blankets half-eaten by mice. Nonie could remember those blankets. They were the ones that were used each year for the shearers when they came, and she had often helped her mother to fold them up and put them away when the shearing contractor and his team had moved on to the next shed.

It was a somewhat eerie experience, recalling that.

She bit her lip. 'What shall we do with them, Ilse?'

'Burn them, I should think. The mice have really been making merry with them, haven't they? This calico is quite good, though, and there's a set of curtains here that could be quite nice if we washed them and starched them up a bit. I think we'll stack all that harness at one end and get Jacey to give his opinion on it. Some of it looks all right if it was done over with neatsfoot to make it supple again, although I don't suppose there's a draughthorse within miles to wear it.'

'And what on earth's that?' Nonie had pulled a large, flat sieve out from underneath the horsecollars and blinkers.

'A prospector's pan?' Ilse shrugged. 'There were a lot of diggings around here at one time, I believe.' She inspected it more closely. 'It's no use, though. See, it's all gone on the bottom. Out it goes!' – and it joined the mounting pile of junk outside the doorway.

Nonie shone her torch into the corner again, stirring the pile gingerly. An item had caught her eye, something else she recognized, even though the lustre of the grained walnut case was obliterated by a thick coating of dust. It was the old carriage clock that had always stood on the mantelpiece in the front hall. It had an ornate brass face, with black enamelled numerals and hands, and at the top there was an antique brass handle for lifting it. Every week of her life her mother used to wind that clock. Every Monday morning, on washday, while she was waiting for the copper to boil.

Nonie brushed away some of the dust with the palm of her hand. Then she stepped under the light, slipped the catch at the back, and pulled it open to get the key to wind it up. Perhaps it still went. Her fingers found the key, and something else as well. A folded piece of paper. It had her mother's name written across it, back and front.

Nonie gazed at it, awestruck, for fully a minute. Then she put the key in its place, snapped the back shut, and set the clock down at her feet. Carefully, with fingers that were suddenly clumsy, she unfolded the paper.

It was a written sheet, and although the ink was a little faded and the paper creamy with age, the words were completely legible. Instinct, rather than familiarity with her father's handwriting, told Nonie that it would be his. The signature – 'Dermot' – at the bottom confirmed the fact.

'My darling' – she read – 'I am more sorry than you will ever know to have to inflict this pain upon you, whom I love more than anything or anyone in this world. By the time you find this I shall have left you, but you will have Wenona, and must be strong for her sake. I've made a lot of wrong decisions for both of us, my darling Alice, but somehow I know that this is the right one. I couldn't tell you, because things were already going so badly on the property anyway, but my last two trips to the city were not to visit the bank's head office at all. The doctor I saw last time said I've a condition for which there's no hope of a cure at this stage, and the specialist in

Sydney confirmed it. Six months at the most. That's not long enough to get us out of the mess I've made, and the only thing I can now spare you and little Nonie is the suffering of watching me getting worse day by day, probably irritable and changed because of the drugs I shall need, and saying and doing things that aren't in my character and that the child would not comprehend. I'd rather be remembered by you both as I am now, but above every other consideration, there's the expense. You will both need what little money we have left, Alice, it would be even further folly on my part to allow it to be squandered on a lost cause. Goodbye, darling, and I pray that you will understand my reasons for taking the step that I am about to take. It will be better this way. God bless you both. I shall love you always. Dermot.'

'What's the matter, Nonie? You look as if you've seen a ghost.'

Nonie folded the piece of paper and put it into the pocket of her jeans, groped her way to the door. She felt that she was going to suffocate.

Outside the sun was getting low in the west. It cast long shadows over the gulleys and through the timber as she made her way, slowly, because she was very tired, up the hill and along the driveway with its avenue of small new trees in their netted enclosures, to the new homestead.

'Nonie! Good gracious, you're as white as a sheet, do you know that? What is it?'

'Is Jacey in, Mrs. Parsons?'

'No, he's not. He shouldn't be long, though. You do look a little under the weather, dear. Are you really feeling all right? How about a cup of tea?'

'I don't think I'll wait.' Nonie felt helpless. She couldn't think properly, wasn't even sure why she was here, now.

'Just a quick cuppa and then you can go,' said the

153

motherly Mrs. Parsons firmly.

'Yes, very well then. Thank you.'

She drank the tea when it came with gratitude. It wasn't too hot, but sweet and strong. She put the cup down again.

'Thanks, Mrs. P., that was lovely.'

'You won't wait for Jacey?'

'No, it doesn't matter. It was nothing really.'

Nonie got up and left the kitchen by the side door. She had walked along the verandah and was crossing the lawn when she heard Jacey's voice. Mrs. Parsons was there too.

'Which way did she go?'

'I don't know, Jacey. Down the drive, I suppose. It was only moments ago that she left.'

'She didn't say why she'd come?'

'She said it didn't matter.'

'Thanks, Mrs. Parsons. I'll have a scout around. Maybe I'll catch up with her.'

Nonie heard the quick, staccato sound of Jacey's elastic-sided boots as they crossed the verandah, and the gauze door creaked as he opened it and closed it after him. Then he came down the front steps and over the lawn towards her.

'Nonie? You wanted to see me?' He peered into her face in the fading light. 'Did you want to see me about something?' he repeated.

She returned his stare a little woodenly.

'It was nothing,' she told him, trying her best to keep that awful weariness out of her voice. 'It doesn't matter, Jacey.'

His hand on her arm prevented her from continuing on her way.

'I think it does,' he contradicted her quietly, his eyes sharpening. 'Come on, we're going back to the house.'

He led her back, over the lawn, up the steps again, and

through the lounge to a room she couldn't remember ever having been shown by Delphine on their rounds of the house. It must be his office, she supposed, small and cosy, with a smell of tobacco and a couple of deep leather chairs and an enormous roll-topped desk with a calendar sitting on the top. There were maps all over the walls. Jacey pushed her gently down into one of the chairs, and Nonie gazed up at him a little blankly.

'I shouldn't have come, Jacey,' she told him defensively. 'I don't know why I did. It was silly.'

'I'll be the judge of that,' said Jacey, and she couldn't help a faint smile at the old, autocratic brusqueness back again. 'I'll get you a drink. You look as if you could do with one.'

'No, thanks – truly. Mrs. P. made me a cup of tea.'

'So she said. What did you want to see me about, then? Is it Pru?' Jacey-like, he came straight to the point.

Nonie fished the note out of her pocket and handed it to him. She fumbled it into his hands with fingers that were surprisingly stiff and cold in spite of the warmth of the evening.

'I found it when Ilse and I were doing out the store,' she heard herself explaining flatly. 'In the back of an old clock. *Our* old clock.'

Jacey took the note and unfolded it, scanned the message quickly. As he read his expression altered subtly, and he went over the contents again more thoroughly. Finally he folded up the note again and put it on the top of the desk. Nonie, waiting, thought she could hardly bear the compassion that was in Jacey's eyes as he turned back from the desk.

'I'm sorry, Nonie,' he said slowly, and his voice was very deep, just a bit gruff. 'And I'm sorry I wasn't here when you came up looking for me.'

And that was the point at which something inside Nonie just seemed to give way. He'd never be there – not for her, anyway – and she'd had no business, no right, to come looking for him, either. Nonie put her head down on the side of Jacey's great padded leather armchair and wept. And once she began, she couldn't seem to stop. She wept for Dermot, for his illness, his loneliness in the secret knowledge of it, his despair. She wept for her mother and the note she'd never got, and for little Pru and poor faithful Stroud who'd done his best to be all a father should, and for patient Ilse and bitter, crippled Raynor and herself and – and – oh, *everything*.

She just cried and cried, with her head buried on her arm.

All the time she wept, Jacey Lomax was squatting down beside her. He made no attempt to stop her, or to touch her, except that just once she felt the roughness of his fingers caressing the soft skin at the nape of her neck. That was the only way she knew he was there at all, until his voice sounded almost in her ear.

'That's right, little one, you have a good cry,' he told her soothingly. 'I reckon you should have done that a long time ago.'

Perversely, when Jacey Lomax told her to do something, she wanted to do exactly the opposite. She seemed to have sobbed herself to a standstill, anyway. She felt drained of emotion, yet somehow relieved too.

'Here, take mine.' Nonie, searching unsuccessfully for her handkerchief, found Jacey's pressed into her hand. When she finally straightened up and pushed back her hair, he abandoned his squatting position and stood up again.

'Still no drink?' She shook her head mutely. 'Cigarette?'

When Nonie shook her head again, he helped himself to a tailor-made one from the box on top of his desk, hitched his trousers and took the other chair. There was silence while his lighter flared.

Jacey drew on his cigarette soberly for a moment or two, and then he spoke again.

'I think you'll feel better when you think about it all from now on, Nonie. I mean later, of course. Just now you've had a pretty tough shock.'

She sighed. 'My mother never found the note, Jacey. She couldn't have bothered to wind the clock every week, afterwards, like she did before my father – went. I suppose the heart just went out of her. It's a pity. It will always be a pity that she didn't know why.'

'I think she probably had a fair idea, Nonie. When a man and a woman love each other they become very close. They often know things, though they may not put them into words, even to each other. They're part of the unspoken, shared experience that comes with living together and loving one another over a period of years. I think, in fact, I'm sure, that your mother knew more than she was able to communicate to you. Remember you were only a child. What, eight years old? Pru's age, no more.'

'I suppose you're right.'

'You think about it. I'm glad you found that note. You can know, can't you, that your father had his own particular brand of courage, after all.'

'I'm grateful to you for saying that, Jacey.' She glanced up at him, at the stern set of his jaw in the brown, craggy face, and the level mouth that, surprisingly, wasn't pronouncing judgment. '*You* wouldn't have taken that way out, though, would you?'

The broad shoulders shrugged. 'I might have.'

'No. I just know you *wouldn't*.' Her voice threatened to crumble again.

'Who can possibly say with honesty what he would do unless he's confronted with an identical set of circumstances? It took guts to do it. We all have decisions to make, and they can't all be the right ones. We've just got to do what we think best. The important thing is to *make* them, to *take* decisions.'

'Yes, I know. One has to *make* them.' Nonie took a deep breath. 'I'm leaving here as soon as ever Ilse and Raynor can get along without me, Jacey. Pru and I. Perhaps you can find another sort of companion for them to take my place.'

Surprise flickered in Jacey's eyes. She could see that, somehow, she had caught him unawares. Just for a moment he seemed to hold his breath. There was a complete stillness about his stance and the way he held the cigarette in mid-air and allowed the smoke to curl in little spirals through his fingers without even moving them, that told her he was making one of those lightning assessments of his. He was watching her all the time he was making it.

'Why did you come up here just now, Nonie? Why to *me*, in particular?'

She shrugged. 'I hardly know why, I just know I shouldn't have. I expect it was because I knew you were the only other person around who actually knew about my relationship to Dermot.'

'Is that the only reason?'

'I just had to tell *somebody*.'

'I don't think this is the time to be making decisions of that sort, Nonie. Not just now. You're overwrought, you know that.'

'No, I'm not. I decided it a while ago. It's not a – a – sudden idea. I've thought it over carefully, from every angle.'

Especially from the angle of Delphine Simpson, she could have told him. Delphine-and-Jacey. How could she possibly stay on there in the house right beneath them, when even his nearness just now was a form of torture?

'Self-inflicted punishment,' she muttered miserably.

'*What* did you say?' His eyes sharpened.

'Nothing, really. I was thinking aloud. But I mean it, Jacey – every word.'

'And what about Pru? You'll be taking her away from everything she has grown to love.'

She shrugged again. 'She'll get over it in time. She's young enough to adapt again.'

'So.' He was quick to pounce, as she might have known he would. He'd been edging her around to this, into a trap. 'It's not Pru who wants to go, it's only you. Why?'

'There's nothing for me here,' she told him dully.

Jacey took her hands and pulled her to her feet to confront him.

'There is, Nonie, you've said so yourself. You're Dermot's daughter, aren't you? Come on, where's that spunk? It can't just have gone, disappeared into thin air? You're going to make a market garden, remember, and renovate the house. You're going to show them all that you can do it.' A pause, because his words didn't seem to be having the effect he'd obviously desired. 'You don't have to buy that old place, Nonie. I don't think I want to sell it, after all. A simple lease for a nominal sum is all I need. It'll give you the same security without the big outlay of capital in an outright purchase. I'll see that your interests are protected when we draw up the lease, you needn't worry about it. Just leave it to me.'

She shook her head. This was almost unbearable, especially now that Jacey was in one of his *persuasive* moods.

'It's very kind of you, Jacey, but no,' she said firmly, staring numbly at the middle button of his shirt which was just about level with her forehead.

Jacey's fingers tipped her chin, took in her widening eyes.

'Don't be frightened of me, Nonie, please,' he ordered crisply. 'You aren't being honest with me, are you? You were really keen on the whole idea not so long ago, and now you're not, even though Pru is settled and happy and it would be the very thing she'd like to happen. What's made you alter your plan so radically? What's changed?'

Nonie's eyes were locked with his. She couldn't seem to drag hers away from Jacey's grey ones, which had gone dark and penetrating and insistent.

'*I've* changed, Jacey, that's what. *I* have.' In spite of her intentions, her composure disintegrated. '*Please*,' she begged brokenly. 'Please don't argue about it, please, Jacey. I – I can't take much more.'

'We'll leave it for now,' he agreed unexpectedly.

'Not just for *now*. For *good*,' she pleaded shakily.

'We'll see,' he would only compromise, gently. 'Come on, Nonie. I'm going to take you home.'

After that she saw little or nothing of him. Whether he was being tactful, giving her time to recover her balance, or whether she had simply gone right out of his mind Nonie had no way of telling, but she was grateful that he hadn't sought her out and raised the matter again.

During the rest of that week and into the next, she and Ilse completed their cleaning-up operations in the store. They burnt the rest of the blankets, threw out everything that was too cracked, old or broken to be of use, and restored as much of the harness as they could, soaking oil into the parched leather and polishing up the tarnished buckles and trappings.

'Some of it's really lovely, isn't it, Ilse?' remarked Nonie a little wistfully. 'Just look at the way this brass has come up. It's so beautifully substantial-looking.'

'Mm, those were the days right enough. They really made things to last. These are greatly prized now, you know. They've suddenly become much sought after for their antique value, like those old Victorian brass bedsteads that we used to think were so awful, and old commodes and the rest.'

'I couldn't collect things just for their rarity, though, could you? I'd have to really like them and want to look at them. I adore these horse brasses, though. I'd love to have a room, a proper harness room like they did in the old days, with all these brasses and collars and blinkers hanging up around the walls, and all the different sizes of horseshoes, the hand-turned kind that the blacksmith used to make himself, and old sulky wheels and snaffles and wooden yokes and maybe even a bellows in the corner, if I could get one, one of those truly huge ones that used to blow up the forge, and – oh, lots of other things.'

Nonie's eyes had gone dreamy. She caught herself up with difficulty.

'Do you smell anything, Ilse?' she asked suddenly, sniffing the air.

'Should I?' Ilse looked up from the top step of the verandah, upon which they had spread out the leather articles on old bits of paper while the oil was soaking in. 'All I can smell is this revolting oil, I'm afraid.'

Nonie wrinkled her nose, stood up.

'I think it's smoke,' she said uncertainly. 'In fact, I'd swear it is.'

At that precise moment the phone rang, and Ilse went off to answer it. When she came back her face was unusually troubled.

'That was Jacey, and yes, it's smoke. There's a fire out on the plains to the west of the town, and he's got to go with the other men to get it under control.'

Nonie's eyes were round.

'Will that be possible, Ilse? It must be a pretty big one for us to be able to smell it from here.'

'It will be if they can get it controlled before it gets to the timber country, and if this breeze doesn't get stronger.' Already Ilse had screwed the cap back on to the oil tin and was wiping her hands on one of the rags. 'Jacey has phoned the school. The children will be quite safe there, Nonie. It's got really wide firebreaks ploughed around it, just like he has up there at the new house. The teacher will keep the children there unless it's quite safe to let them go by the time school's out, and Pru is to go up to Jacey's house. Hattie will be up there with Mrs. Parsons, anyway, to man the telephone while Jacey's away and prepare supplies for the beaters.'

'And what about here?' Nonie asked dubiously, glancing around at the decaying weatherboards and ant-eaten verandah posts.

Ilse pulled a wry face.

'I've told Jacey we'll stay meantime. The way it's heading now, it's almost parallel with the creek and so we could just be lucky. He says we've not to leave it too late, though. If the worst happens, I'm to have the car out, so we can go up to his place if we need to.'

'I see. Is there anything else we can do?'

Ilse shook her head.

'Not really, unless I were to take Raynor up to Jacey's house and leave him there with the women and children. And I can't do that to him, Nonie. At least he feels he's in charge here, and that he has some sort of useful role to play. You can imagine how miserably frustrated he is knowing perfectly well that all the other men, the able-bodied ones, have gone off to the fire-front.'

Yes, she could imagine how he must feel, thought Nonie, as she went to collect the eggs from the hen-run. She felt helpless enough herself, but glad of the few small duties she could think of to do.

The waiting was the worst. Cinders drifted past on the breeze, and as the morning wore on they became thicker, larger, and the smell of burning increased.

They ate a salad lunch almost in silence, all three aware of a sense of strain. The surrounding bush was almost lost in a blue haze that intensified in the early afternoon. The heightening breeze lifted it past the house in ever-changing density.

When Nonie climbed to the top of the tankstand she could now see a great orange cloud in the sky on the other side of the scrub. One could only conjecture the hold that the fire must have to make such a widespread glow as that, and her heart went out to the teams of men who were fighting the battle to deflect it in its path towards the timber. To Jacey, and the others.

Now she could catch the roar of it above the trees, and even as she looked a tongue of flame leapt high into the air and then another. The roar was louder, a background now to the staccato crackle of burning wood and leaves. The fire must have eaten up the big body of grass out on the plain, and was licking into the scrub. The timber had caught.

Nonie scrambled down the iron ladder that ran up the side of the water-tank, and hurried around the side of the house.

Ilse and Raynor were watching from the lawn.

'It's come,' she said. 'It's into the trees.'

'Yes, it's caught,' repeated Raynor, fiercely, helplessly. 'God, if only I wasn't so blasted *useless*, tied to this damn contraption. Nonie, get me the hose, and connect it to that tap, will you?'

'What are you going to do?'

'I'll soak the verandah boards and uprights. It's worth a chance.'

'But it won't touch the *house*, will it?'

'With the wind where it is, it could,' he replied grimly. 'Get going, girl. We won't let the old place go without at least the semblance of a fight.'

She ran, then, to do as he had asked her, watched as he started to wheel himself up and down, playing the jet of water over the perimeter of the rambling structure.

'It *is* heading this way, Raynor,' she told him breathlessly, after another scramble up and down the tankstand. 'What can we do, Ilse and I? We can't just stand there and – and let it come.'

'We may have to yet. You can get a ladder and block up the down-pipes, Nonie. Go right around the house. Use those old tennis-balls in the chest in the hall, or stuff them with wads of cloths, anything. Ilse, fill as many buckets of water as you can and bring them out and pass them up to Nonie. We'll run water into as much of the guttering as we've time for. It could just stop the building catching.'

'Yes, Raynor.'

They worked like beavers, breathlessly, in silence. Nonie was glad of the intense activity. The heat was now oppressive, and each roar of flame and crash of branches was followed by a bursting shower of sparks sent skywards.

'That's it, Raynor,' Ilse was gasping, her face flame-coloured itself. 'What else?'

'It's all we can do, Ilse, but wait.' His voice was taut. 'We could still be lucky.'

'I think I should get you into the car, Ray.'

'No, we'll wait a bit yet. Jacey was right. It's running parallel to the creek. If it misses the house, we'll need to be here anyway, to put out any side-spread that could still threaten it. There's always the water to retreat to, anyway.'

'Ray, Jacey *said*.'

'You *hear* me, Ilse,' barked Raynor, with a good hint of the old Lomax bossiness.

They waited and watched, too tense to speak again. Nonie never knew afterwards how long they waited before Raynor said, on a note of elation, 'We're going to be in the clear. The wind has veered a little, look. It's taking it away a bit. By God, it's like a miracle!'

But the miracle was short-lived. As the top of one of the lofty, blazing ironbarks broke off, it fell through the air in a veritable shower of sparks and crackling twigs, and the next moment the old wattle-tree was alight. From there on it was almost inevitable that the homestead's frail timber, so close, so very close, would be next.

'Raynor, *no*!' Nonie was hardly aware that the agonized shriek of protest was hers.

'That's it, Nonie, I'm afraid. It's going to rip through there like lightning now.'

Nonie ran up the steps and along the verandah.

The west wing was well alight. She could hear the steamy hissing of the flames licking the wetness out of the wood that Raynor had spent so much effort in soaking. They had taken a proper grip, and the water had evaporated altogether in the intense heat by the time she dragged her old tin trunk outside and dumped it on the lawn. On her way back past the piles of harness that she and Ilse had been working on, she stopped to fling all that out over the verandah rail too, piece by piece – and then the heat was too much, and she was forced back, down the steps again.

'Come out of that, Nonie, for heaven's sake! Do you want to be burnt alive?' Raynor shouted in some irritation.

Nonie came back obediently to Ilse and Raynor to find that Delphine had joined them. Beside their own grimy persons she seemed like a creature from another planet, fresh and clean in a buttercup-yellow linen dress. Except for the fact that some of the flying cinders had settled on her hair and shoulders, and that her feet were bare and a little slimy because she had waded across the shallowest bit of the creek, she was dressed for a stroll down Martin Place.

'I left my car on the other side of the water,' she explained, flicking off some of the smuts from the yellow linen, and slipping with a small grimace of distaste into the white sandals she had been carrying in her hand. 'Hadn't you better come up to the other house now? Those were Jacey's clear instructions, as I understand it.'

'We're safe enough here, Delphine. The wind is taking the fire away from us now. We're behind it here, or as good as. There's nothing more we can do, though. Things just didn't go our way, that's all.'

The defeated twist to Raynor's mouth, the bitter frustration in his voice were too much for Nonie to bear. She couldn't just stand there like the others, watching Raynor watching the house burning. Anything was better than that!

She slipped away with a couple of the buckets, the ones that she and Ilse had been using earlier to run water into the guttering, and took them down to the creek to fill them, intending to douse the few spoils she had salvaged on the side lawn. The tin trunk should survive all right, but the harness would stand a better chance to withstand small flying bits of burning wood if she covered it over with some wetted sacks. One or two good-sized sparks could easily set the thick checked woollen felt padding on those old horsecollars and saddles alight. She might as well do her best for them seeing that she had thrown them there.

Nonie clambered down the steepest part of the bank, and let each pail sink slowly into the water until it was brimfull. Then she began to carry them back, but this time up the proper pathway, because the gradient was easier and she had a fair load. Every now and then the water slopped out over her legs, so there was no point in hurrying too much with them. When she reached the top again, and came into full view of the blazing house, Nonie put down the buckets and stared. She stared in a sort of mesmerized horror because she thought she must be having a nightmare.

Delphine and Ilse were still standing on the lawn, and they were looking towards the house, and there, coming out of the house, framed for an instant in the burning doorway, were Raynor and Jacey.

It could only be Jacey. Nonie knew so well the set of his shoulders, his narrow-hipped, tall figure in the khaki bush-shirt and that awful old hat. And Raynor beside him, almost as tall, nearly as broad, was propping Jacey up as they came clumsily down the steps and back over the grass.

Raynor was propping *Jacey* up?

Raynor was *walking*?

Nonie rubbed her eyes to see if the vision would disappear. It didn't. Like a slow-motion movie, the two men crossed the lawn, still clutching each other, and when they reached the foot of the box-gum at the edge of the grass Raynor put one hand against its stout bole and allowed Jacey to sink gently down at his feet.

Nonie picked up the pails again and ran, abandonedly, with water spilling and slopping as she went. By the time she got there Ilse and Delphine were already kneeling beside Jacey. Raynor was still leaning against the trunk of the tree at whose base his brother was slumped. He was breathing heavily. In answer to Nonie's agonized, unspoken question, he gasped,

'He's O.K., Nonie – he – thought you were – *in* there. Didn't – even – *ask*—'

She put her arms around him and hugged him, her eyes brimming with tears that didn't actually fall because she was too full of wonder even to think of crying just then.

'Raynor, you're walking! Don't you realize what you've done? You're *walking*! Ray, we've got our miracle after all!'

Raynor had regained his breath. His gaunt features split in a rueful grin.

'And it'll be another miracle if I ever get away from this tree. I reckon I'm pretty well wedded to the damn thing. Here, give us a hand, will you, Nonie. I've a feeling that if I let go I might fall over.'

She placed her arm firmly about his waist. 'No, you won't, Raynor,' she asserted confidently. 'There's no going back now. You've got it made. Let's go now.'

Together they walked a few steps, jubilantly.

'Nonie?' That was Ilse. Ilse was calling to her from where she knelt beside Jacey's recumbent form. 'Please, Nonie, could you come?' she called softly, but with an underlying sense of urgency that caused Raynor to turn around and meet her eyes. There was no mistaking the message in those beautiful blue eyes of Ilse's. The message was for Raynor alone, and even Raynor couldn't mistake it this time. As Nonie dropped down beside Jacey Raynor took Ilse into his arms and embraced her quietly. Then they walked slowly away together, and each painful step seemed to Nonie to be a step of triumph.

Jacey's face, when Nonie looked down at him, was almost unrecognizable. Her heart gave a lurch. His eyes were closed, and even the lids looked red and sore. His forehead and cheeks were blackened, his neck was smothered in soot and cinders, and the bush-shirt was spattered with masses of raggedy holes. There was an angry burn up his left forearm from wrist to elbow, and behind his left ear a small trickle of blood was already congealing.

Nonie gazed at it in awe.

'I thought Ray said he was *all right*?' she said to Delphine in a strangled voice that she could scarcely recognize.

'He will be, Nonie, though why you had to disappear like that and send him looking for you goodness only

168

knows. Now look what you've done!' She relented at the sight of Nonie's stricken expression. 'He was conscious when Raynor and he came out,' she told her grudgingly. 'A falling beam caught him on the side of the head just before they got through the doorway.'

'What can we do?'

'The doctor will be here shortly. Jacey had phoned for him and an ambulance from his house before he came down. He expected to find you all up there, and when he didn't, and saw the place ablaze as well, he thought something must have gone badly wrong. You knew well enough what his instructions were.'

Oh, Jacey. Darling Jacey. What had she done? What had they *all* done?

Nonie stood up, rubbed the grass from her knees and carried over the water she had brought. Then she took her handkerchief and dipped it in and began, very gently, to wash away the soot and grime from Jacey's face. It was a pitifully small scrap of handkerchief, but it served the purpose not too badly. The pallor that was revealed by her ministrations smote Nonie afresh. The colour that normally ran healthily beneath Jacey's heavy tan had drained away, leaving his complexion a ghostly, ghastly yellow.

It was all their fault – hers, especially – for not doing what he had ordered in the first place!

Nonie got the other bucket of water, and eased Jacey's burned arm into it, running the water through the small piece of cloth she had, to the place where the water couldn't quite reach, up near his elbow.

'I hope you know what you're doing?' remarked Delphine with some asperity. She had thus far watched in complete silence.

'I think so. I read it somewhere.'

The coolness of the water on his burning arm seemed to waken Jacey. He opened his eyes and gazed up at

Nonie with an expression that was quite blank at first and then, with returning recollection, somewhat sharper.

'Where's Raynor?' he asked faintly.

'With Ilse, walking. They went down to the creek.'

'Good.'

He closed his eyes again, then opened them as another thought seemed to occur to him. He raised his head a little, reached out with his good hand, and took Nonie's wet one in a firm grasp.

'Don't run out on me, just when I need you, will you?' he said, and although his voice was still faded and hoarse and not like Jacey's at all, the words themselves were quite distinct.

'No, Jacey, I won't,' she promised, but it was doubtful if he heard her, because already his grasp had slackened as he slid into unconsciousness again.

'I wish the doctor would hurry up,' said Delphine impatiently. 'I think Jacey's out of his mind with that blow on the head. Concussion, probably.'

'I think so too,' agreed Nonie.

And it was the only point upon which she had seemed to have agreed with Delphine Simpson during their entire acquaintance!

CHAPTER EIGHT

THE sound of voices and footsteps making their way up the bank aroused Jacey once more. By the time the doctor arrived at his side, followed by two ambulance-men carrying a stretcher, his eyes were open again, and he lifted his head and tried to sit up.

'Lie back, Jacey, and let me look you over, you mutt,' the doctor told him with what seemed to Nonie a total lack of respect. He gave his patient a little push that sent him flat again, and chuckled. 'I must say this is the first time a feller has ever phoned and sent for me before he's even *had* his accident. Warning in advance, so to speak. You must be psychic!'

Jacey grinned sheepishly. 'Far from psychic,' he replied with a certain quiet irony. 'There wasn't anyone *in* there, as it turned out!'

The doctor was checking his eyes and the contused swelling on the side of his head. Finally he sat back on his heels.

'You've most certainly had a fair wallop there, Jacey. You must have a skull of cast iron. I can't detect any signs of concussion, but that's not to say it mightn't be delayed, though. We'll take you in, anyway, and keep an eye on you for a bit.' He was snipping away at the armhole of the tattered shirt while he was speaking, pulling the cloth aside as he cut it. 'This will need attention too.'

'You can do it up at the house, can't you? I'm not going in just now.'

'You'd better.'

'I'm not. I've things to see to.' Jacey struggled to a sitting position.

The doctor sighed. 'Have it your way, Jacey. I know

171

you too well to waste time in arguing. At least let these blokes take you up there, just to prove to themselves, if to no one else, that their journey was really necessary. You're in a shocked condition, so you might as well let them save you a little unnecessary exertion, and you needn't try to pretend that you're feeling any too great. You can't be.'

Jacey gave a wan smile. He was even paler than he'd been before, now that he was sitting up.

'See what I mean?' The doctor pressed home his advantage. 'Anyway, why should we *all* get our feet wet? We're over the other side of the creek, so you'd need to wade it. The fire's burning out, by the way, Jacey. Your own fire-breaks have it cornered, but there was still too much smoke around to chance the main road.'

'You kept to the other side of the water?'

'We did.'

'I see.' He considered a moment. 'Where's your car, Delphine?'

'It's over there too. I'll take it up to the house.'

'You might give Nonie here a lift up with you,' Jacey said to the doctor as he allowed the men to move him on to the stretcher with a reasonably good grace. 'Where's my hat?' he asked in afterthought, from his prone position.

'If you mean this—' The doctor picked it up with an expression of disgust.

'That's it.'

'It's sopping wet. What did they do, pour a bucket of water over you to bring you round?'

Jacey's lips quirked.

'I dipped it in the horse-trough on my way down. Part of the old fire-drill. Habit dies hard.'

'Hmm. Maybe it's a good thing it does. It no doubt helped deflect that rafter a bit when it hit you.'

'That's right,' agreed Jacey calmly, placing the hat

over his eyes to keep out the glare from the sky. 'Everything's jake now. I can't think straight if I haven't got my hat. As I said, habit dies hard.'

'Let's go, then.'

They moved in slow procession over the grass and down the path to the shallow part of the creek. On the other side the men put Jacey into the ambulance and drove off, Delphine following in her yellow Lotus. Nonie and the doctor brought up the rear.

'So you're Nonie, eh?' He reached across her to pull the passenger door shut. 'I was wondering when I'd be meeting you. I've heard a lot about you from Jacey.'

'What?' Nonie looked at him, startled.

'Nothing bad, don't worry! Nor am I speaking professionally, now, when I say that, but as a friend of the Lomaxes – a personal friend. We're good mates, Jacey and I. I've known him for more years than I care to remember.'

'Oh, I see.' Nonie opened her palm to find her white handkerchief still clutched in her hand – a tepid, sodden little ball of cloth, and not white any more, either. She gazed down at it a moment, and then began to unfold it, spreading it out carefully upon one knee as they drove. 'Will he really be all right?'

'Who? Jacey?' He sensed her need for reassurance. 'He's as tough as they come, you must have seen that for yourself. We'll keep him in bed for twenty-four hours, just in case of concussion. The burns will take longer to get right, of course. One's fairly major, and I've no doubt it's giving him hell, although he'd be the last to admit it.'

'I feel it's mostly my fault that it happened.'

'You mustn't feel that.' He glanced over, took in the strain in her voice, the tenseness as she sat there smoothing the edges of the little hankie with unnecessary attention. 'You've no need to feel that way, it's the very last

173

thing Jacey would want. And anyway,' he added bracingly, 'look at the good that's come out of it. Raynor is walking.'

'Yes, that, at least, is wonderful.'

'I've had the idea for a long time that there was some emotional block to his total recovery, some mental reason rather than a medical one, for his progress being arrested. It took something big to shake him out of it, and Jacey unwittingly provided it.'

'I still don't know what happened.'

'I do, or the bare bones of it, anyway. I met Raynor and Ilse on their way up to the other house. I couldn't believe my eyes when I saw Raynor was actually walking, but I couldn't spare the time to stop and yarn about it beyond telling him he'd done enough for one day. He told me about Jacey, seemed pretty shattered by the whole experience. He said Jacey came around the corner of the house. He was looking over to where they were all standing and then he just plunged inside. It was only when Raynor heard him shouting your name that he looked around and saw you weren't standing with them any longer. He knew you weren't inside the house, wherever else you might be, but Jacey obviously thought you were, so he had to act fast. He said he doesn't even remember getting out of the chair and going after him, but he got the message across inside, and they were just coming out again when Jacey got clobbered by that falling beam.'

'It really *was* my fault, then, but I'm glad about Raynor, and so will Jacey be. He'll think it was worth it.'

'Yes, I'm sure he will,' agreed the man beside her comfortingly. 'I'll see you later, then,' he added, for they had drawn up at the front of the new homestead and the men were carrying Jacey inside.

The doctor followed them into the hallway and through to the bedroom, and Nonie found herself left on the side verandah with Delphine.

'Excuse me a moment, I must go and wash my feet. These sandals will be quite ruined, I'm afraid.' Delphine regarded them fastidiously. 'Don't go away before I come back, will you, though, Nonie. I want a word with you.'

Left alone on the verandah, Nonie wondered where Delphine thought she would be likely to go away *to* right now, anyway.

From here she could see the smouldering ruins of the old house down below her. Every now and then a flame wriggled out of the smoking heaps of rubble which were all that were now left of the place. Ironically, the out-houses were still intact. The engine-shed, the chook yards hadn't been touched by the fire at all. The wind had veered enough to save them at the last moment – the house, too, if it hadn't been for the old wattle-tree catching alight like that.

Nonie sat back with her eyes closed, thinking. She was still reliving the horrible moment when they'd known the old building was finally doomed. She could still hear the roar as the flames took hold, and her nostrils still stung with the acrid fumes of the smoke that had billowed up in such great, dense gusts.

A sound brought her back to the present.

'That's better.' Delphine had returned. 'I couldn't wait to get that nasty slimy mud off. I didn't bother putting my sandals back on, though. I shall throw them away when I get home. I happened to have a pair of driving shoes in the car, so I've put them on instead.' She stretched out a shapely leg to inspect her neatly shod foot.

'I've been thinking, while you were off just now. It's wonderful about Raynor, isn't it?' Nonie said a little shyly. She always found herself ill at ease when she was alone with Delphine. 'It was strange the way it happened, the way it all worked out.'

'Yes. That's partly what I wanted to speak to you about,' Delphine replied matter-of-factly. 'Now that Raynor is walking again, there's no need for you to remain, is there? Your services can be dispensed with after this.'

'Yes, I expect that's so.'

'And they've nowhere even to put you up, with the house burned from under their feet. You'll be something of an embarrassment to them in the circumstances – you and the child.'

'Yes, I realize that too, Delphine.' Nonie was beginning to feel a hot, uncomfortable flush seeping into her cheeks. 'I'm as aware of it as you are, I can assure you. I've no intention that we should embarrass them, though. I'll make arrangements to relieve them of our presence just as soon as I can.'

'Good. I'm glad you regard the situation in such a sensible light, Nonie.' Delphine paused. 'As a matter of fact, I'd like to help. I can give you a lift back in to town right now.'

'Oh, you mustn't think of doing that.'

'Nonsense, it will be a pleasure. My car is here anyway. If you get the child we can go right now, and we'll collect that old trunk you rescued on the way. That's another thing – and I don't want you to be hurt or offended at my mentioning it. You won't have much left in the way of clothes, either of you, will you? I can give you some of mine when we get to town, and I'd like to buy you some more to set you off again. And for Pru, of course.'

'Why would you want to do that?' Nonie couldn't help asking in some surprise. She had never found Delphine quite so friendly or sympathetic before!

'One wants to be neighbourly, doesn't one? It could just as easily have been me and my things that were affected in a fire.' Delphine shrugged. 'If it had been, I'd be appreciative if someone offered to do the same for me.'

'No, I couldn't allow you to do *that*, thank you, Delphine.' Nonie sounded quite shocked. 'I have enough money in the bank to take care of both of us, although of course I'll have to be sparing with it. I hadn't counted on a disaster of this sort, exactly. We don't need a lot of clothes, though. I'll get us the bare minimum in the meantime. I prefer to be independent, but I do thank you all the same.'

'Well, at least you'll allow me to pay your fares down to Sydney, or wherever it is you'll be going. We can get you on to the plane or the train, whichever you prefer. Tonight, if you like, if it's the train. You must see for yourself that there are far too many people in this house already just now – Ilse and Raynor, and Mrs. Parsons *and* Hattie. We're simply not needed, you and I, and as for Pru, children are in the way at a time like this. In fact I'm even feeling a little bit *de trop* myself at present. There can be too many women around, all getting under each other's feet, don't you agree?'

She stood up, smoothed the yellow linen down over her hips and seat.

'Come then, Nonie. I shall drive you both into town.'

Nonie hesitated.

'I'd like to say good-bye to Jacey first, Delphine. He's been – well, kind. I'd just *like* to say it, if you don't mind?' Her voice thickened, because there seemed to be a lump in her throat that prevented the words from coming out properly. She knew they had to go, she'd known it for weeks now, so the sooner the better. She dreaded having to see Jacey again. She wondered how she could bear it, actually *saying* good-bye, but it had to be done, and she'd manage it somehow, just as she'd always managed to do things that had to be done. It was the only honourable way, even though it would be for her the most difficult and painful task of her entire life.

Delphine seemed to sense the struggle that Nonie was

having with herself.

'You don't have to see him at all, Nonie. What nonsense! You can always write and thank him. I shall personally see that any salary due to you is forwarded on. Indeed I shall pay you what is owing to you, with a comfortable margin, before I see you off. If you don't hurry we shall miss the train.' She was beginning to sound impatient.

'I promised.' Nonie's eyes were full of tears. They blurred her vision, and made Delphine's figure just a fuzzy yellow shape in front of her.

'Come *at once*, do you hear me?' Delphine's voice rose peremptorily. 'Come now, and get the child too. As usual you quite overrate your importance, Nonie, and forget that you're a mere employee. Good-byes are quite unnecessary, so forget that rubbish and get a move on.'

'Indeed good-byes are unnecessary, because there aren't going to be any.'

Jacey's voice, deep, a little hoarse, but slow and clear, sounded from somewhere behind them. He was propping himself up in the doorway, and save for his unearthly pallor he appeared to be the old Jacey back again – in a clean shirt and trousers, sporting a heavy white bandage right up his left arm, which was supported in a neat calico sling. The doctor was hovering behind him as he stepped out on to the verandah.

'Jacey!' Delphine swung around. 'How long have you been there?'

'Long enough.' He sounded – and looked! – unbelievably grim. 'Come here, Nonie.'

'Jacey?'

'Come here, Nonie. Just do as I say. You are *not* going to say good-bye, do you hear me? You are *not* going to town with Delphine. You are *not* going to run away, or even try to. You are going to remain here. You are going to stay here with me and do me the honour of becoming

178

my wife.'

'Your wife?' echoed Nonie, in the very faintest of voices.

'My wife,' repeated Jacey firmly. 'Come here.'

He put out his hand imperiously, and Nonie found herself obeying him, wordlessly. His fingers closed over hers in a warm, commanding clasp.

Delphine shrugged from the doorway.

'If and when you recover your senses, Jacey, give me a ring, will you?' she managed in acid tones.

'Thank you, Delphine, but I'm perfectly in command of my senses, never more so.'

For the first time, at the sober firmness of his voice and expression, she faltered just a little. 'Then there's nothing more to be said, is there?'

'Not so far as you're concerned,' he replied, with uncompromising politeness.

'Then I'll wish you all the luck in the world, darling – and I think you'll need it,' she couldn't resist adding spitefully. 'Remember you'll be taking on that kid as well.'

'I'm well aware of what I intend taking on, thanks, Delphine. Now please go.'

And she did, with a furious slamming of the gauze door as she ran down the steps. Seconds later, the Lotus engine revved viciously, and in a shower of flying gravel it went spurting off down the drive.

Jacey let go of Nonie's hand and sat down heavily in the nearest chair. There were beads of sweat on his forehead and his breathing was noticeably uneven, but as the doctor leaned over him in concern he actually grinned, and the doctor started to laugh.

'That was more of a statement than a proposal, Jacey, I reckon, but may I be the first to wish you every happiness, *and* mean it?' He gave a mock whistle. 'Phew! What a virago Delphine can be when she gets going! I can quite see why you insisted on staying on your feet till you'd got the thing sorted out to your satisfaction, old chap, but *now* will you let me get you into bed and give you a shot of something for that arm? For a prospective bridegroom you're in abominable shape.' He turned to Nonie, still standing there in a frozen state with a wide-eyed look about her. 'You aren't going to turn him down *now*, I suppose, at this stage? You won't *really* run out on him, like he's kept saying you would?'

She shook her head stupidly, trying to bring herself back to reality.

'I won't run out.'

'Good girl! Then give me ten minutes with him, Nonie, and after that he's all yours.'

The doctor hauled Jacey to his feet again and would have propelled him towards the bedroom, except that Jacey stopped once more when he was passing Nonie.

'It wasn't much of a proposal, Nonie,' he told her in an unabashed, husky voice, and passion blazed quite shamelessly in his eyes as he looked down at her for a moment. 'We'll have to regard it as a trial run. I'll do better the second time round, when we're alone.'

She nodded, felt his lips just brush her forehead before he went inside.

The doctor was more than ten minutes with Jacey, but when he came back he seemed well pleased.

'I've given him something for the pain from those burns, and he should be asleep shortly, so make it snappy if you want to get some sense out of him.'

'I will.' She hesitated. 'I won't know what to say to him,' she confessed shyly. 'I mean, I never dreamed – I didn't know – I thought that he and Delphine—'

He looked at her sharply.

'Delphine? Nonsense! He's been in love with you for months, I've known that by the way he spoke about you. I'm not wrong, believe me. I know Jacey Lomax better than most people do, and it's the first time I've seen him uncertain how to handle a situation. He must be slipping!' He couldn't resist a chuckle. 'He had this notion that you didn't like him. Said something about having to buy some time to work you around to the idea. I think you're going to be good for Jacey, do you know that.' He patted her kindly on the shoulder. 'Go on in there and cheer him up. He keeps thinking you're going to do a disappearing act, so he can't be too sure of you even yet. I'll see you both tomorrow. I'll have to go and find Raynor now.'

When Nonie went into Jacey's room, she was surprised to find that he wasn't in bed at all, but merely stretched out on top of the counterpane with a couple of pillows slung behind his head.

Lying there in his open-necked shirt and pale drill trousers, with the plaster dressing on the side of his head and his eyes closed, he appeared boyish and – in a way that Nonie could not have explained – vulnerable.

At the sound of her step Jacey opened his eyes and invited her to come in. She advanced timidly.

'I thought you'd be in bed, Jacey – properly, I mean. Shouldn't you be?'

'I'm resting, so it amounts to the same thing. There are a few things I want to see to later, and I've a couple of phone calls to make. I didn't intend to opt out of the fire-fighting activities quite so suddenly.' He smiled. A rather pale and weary smile, it was, and his mouth lifted somewhat satirically at one corner as he looked across at her. 'It wasn't a very dignified exit, was it?'

'Not very. It was a brave thing to do, Jacey. Just what one would expect of *you*, but foolish too. And all my fault,' she added bitterly.

'Come here, Nonie, and sit on the bed beside me.'

As she obeyed, Jacey put his good arm around her and drew her against him, pressing her head against his shirt. She could feel his breath on her brow, his lips near her cheek.

'I thought you were in there.' He murmured the words into her hair in a voice so deep and full of despair that what he was saying was barely distinguishable. 'I thought you were in there. I thought you were *in* there.' He seemed to be torturing himself by saying it aloud.

'I know, Jacey. I'm sorry. If anything had happened to you because of me—' She stopped, unable to continue.

He put her away from him, studying her face intently.

'Would you have cared, Nonie? Would you?'

Jacey's eyes held a strange, searching glitter.

'Of course I'd have cared. How can you even ask such a thing?'

'I find I can ask it with some justification,' he replied, inscrutability returning. 'You'd have gone, wouldn't you, there with Delphine just now? *Wouldn't* you?'

'Yes,' she admitted lamely, dropping her eyes.

'Why?'

'Jacey, please. Can't we leave it, for now at least? You're supposed to be quiet. You're supposed to be asleep.'

'And while I'm asleep you'll doubtless by thinking of all sorts of evasions and half-truths to fob me off with.'

'I *won't*. I don't *want* to fob you off.' Nonie blushed fierily.

'I want the truth, Nonie, and I want it now.' Jacey's tone was relentless. 'Why would you have gone with Delphine?'

'Because I thought – I thought—'

'What did you think?'

'That you and Delphine – that you—' She searched for the right words, but it was impossible to find them.

'That we—?' He waited, and when he saw that she wasn't going to continue, he actually said it for her. 'That there was some sort of understanding between us, was that it?'

She nodded miserably. 'Yes, that was it. *I* knew it all along. I knew it was Delphine, even though Raynor said it wasn't. *He* said it was Ilse.'

'Ilse? Ilse!' Jacey exclaimed, startled into a sitting position on the bed. 'Good God, who am I supposed to be? Don Juan and Casanova rolled into one?' He ran frenzied fingers through his hair and swung his legs over the edge of the bed. 'What the hell do you mean, *Ilse?*' he demanded agitatedly, in supreme exasperation.

'Jacey, *please*. Lie down, please.'

'Not till you explain, I won't. Ilse! Dear lord in heaven!' he muttered perplexedly.

'Lie down, Jacey.'

'I can't, not till I know. What the devil have you all been hatching up?'

'I've no intention of explaining until you lie down again, Jacey Lomax,' Nonie told him with a calm that she wasn't actually feeling.

Finally, seeing that she truly meant it, he lay back against the pillows again with a sigh of resignation.

'I don't think that all this discussion is good for you,' she offered uncertainly, taking in his drawn appearance and the fact that he had closed his eyes again.

He brushed that aside impatiently.

'Never mind whether it's good or bad. We'd better get the record straight while we're at it. Get on with it, Nonie. What about Ilse?'

So Nonie told him. She repeated word for word the conversation that Raynor had overheard, and had related, in turn, to her.

'I'm beginning to see,' said Jacey thoughtfully, when she had finished. 'That poor devil of a brother of mine! Poor Ray. If only he'd *said* something, brought it out into the open. Do you know what we were actually talking about, Nonie?'

She shook her head.

'We were talking about the fact that he probably wouldn't walk again. At that time, you see, the doctors thought the outlook was hopeless. It was many weeks afterwards before they concluded that the problem was now an emotional one, because in other directions he had made unexpectedly favourable progress. One didn't know *when* to tell him, or *what* to tell him, but in the early days the situation was quite clear-cut – they thought the shock of knowing that his legs were possibly permanently damaged might set him back irreparably. He was in no condition for the truth. I had to beg Ilse to try to pretend, somehow, that all was well, that things were just the same as before. For his sake, we waited till they deemed him fit enough to hear it.'

'There was something else too.'

'Was there?' Jacey's grey eyes had sharpened. 'What else, Nonie?'

She traced the checked pattern on the bed-cover with one finger, gazing at it.

'You kissed Ilse then, too, Jacey. You had your arms around her, and you were kissing her, and Raynor saw that too.'

'Yes, I believe I did. I *kissed* her, I wasn't *kissing* her. There's a difference, Nonie. I was comforting her, nothing more. I'll have to have a yarn with Ray about it some time.'

'He'll understand, Jacey. I told him there'd be an explanation, if only he could bring himself to seek one from you.'

'It was a kiss of comfort, of consolation, nothing more. I hoped that Ilse could draw some strength, some encouragement, from a little brotherly support.'

'Yes, I know. I *told* Raynor it'd be that sort of kiss.'

His lips twitched, although he still lay there with his eyes shut.

'You certainly seem to have discussed some surprising

topics with brother Raynor. You sound quite an authority on kisses, too,' he murmured drowsily.

She flushed. 'Well, I know there are different sorts, for different reasons.'

The flush deepened, painfully, as she remembered the kiss *she* had once received from Jacy too.

With uncanny perception he seemed to have read her mind.

'Yes, Nonie,' he said, and his voice was a very soft, deep murmur, nothing more. 'There are different sorts, for different reasons.'

Jacey still had his eyes shut, but he was drawing her towards him again, inexorably, and there was a slow, delicious anticipation about the way he did it that set Nonie's heart racing. When he opened his eyes and looked at her, there was no anger in Jacey's darkening gaze, not like that other time, and when his lips found hers they were gentle, fleeting. It was the merest butterfly of a kiss, right on her mouth.

'I'm sorry about that other time, Nonie,' he murmured, his lips at her temple. 'I was so angry. How can I ever make you understand? I was angry that you didn't trust me enough to confide in me who you really were. I knew, sure, but I still hoped that *you* would tell me yourself. I've loved you almost since the first time I saw you, when you and Pru were standing there in the half-dark by the old wattle-tree looking like a couple of lost and frightened kids. If you only knew how many times I've longed to take you in my arms and kiss you and transfer all those worries and troubles of yours into *my* care and *my* keeping.'

'Jacey, I didn't know.' Nonie gazed at him, a mixture of incredulity and astonishment. She was longing to believe what he was telling her right now. Longing to, but hardly daring to.

'I just couldn't seem to get through to you. You were so independent I just got nowhere and I thought I'd go crazy with the sheer frustration of it.'

'But, Jacey, I didn't know. How could I *know*?'

'We always seemed to be striking sparks off each other, and the situation never seemed right for telling you how I felt. And then you said you were going to leave as soon as Raynor and Ilse could get along without you, and I knew then that you would never feel for me the way I was feeling about you.'

'But I did, Jacey. I do. I love you, I love you.'

'I reckoned, though, that if I could somehow buy some more time, I'd *make* you care, I'd *make* you love me, just a little bit. Goodness knows how I was going to do it, but I certainly had to keep you here somehow.'

'Jacey, *darling* Jacey, you didn't have to *make* me.'

'No? There's nothing for me here, you said. Those were your very own words, Nonie.'

'*Because* I cared,' she told him urgently. '*Because* I loved you. I couldn't stay down there at the bottom of the valley with you and Delphine up here, not possibly. How could I, loving you as I do? I knew I'd have to go when I – when she – well, I just knew I'd have to, because life would have been too unbearable being so close to you and unable to share things with you, having to watch you sharing your life with someone else and unable ever to let you suspect in the smallest degree how I felt.'

'She said something to you, didn't she? Delphine? Something pretty positive, it must have been, to make you so unswerving in your decision to go. You don't have to answer if you don't want to, Nonie. I *know* she did, and I heard enough out there on the verandah to make doubly sure that my suspicions weren't unfounded. Dear heaven! I wish I could think straight.' He passed a weary hand over his eyes. 'That damned drug of Trevor's just adds to the muddle. Look here, Nonie, it seems to me, if I hadn't gone out there on to the verandah just now and stopped you, you'd have walked right out of my life.'

'Only because I loved you. Only because I didn't *know*.'

'Hmm. And where would you have gone, for interest?'

'I don't know. I hadn't really thought about where.'

'Well, wherever it was I'd have found you. I'd have tracked you down and brought you back and made you learn how to love me.'

'I love you already, Jacey, I don't have to learn how. I couldn't love you more than I do. It's the most tender, wonderful, painful thing that's ever happened to me. The only greater pain would be leaving you.'

'You won't, will you, Nonie? You *will* marry me, be my wife? Trevor was right, it was one hell of a strange proposal out there on the verandah. I muffed the thing a bit, but I had to stop you leaving at all costs, and I hadn't time to consider any finesse. There were too many people around, and anyhow, I didn't know, then, how *you* felt, either. I just had to take a chance on it. Will you be my wife, please, Nonie?'

'If that's what you really want.'

'Want? Good lord, what does one do to convince you?' He kissed her then, long and tenderly and wonderfully, with a quiet, possessive skill that caused Nonie to cling to him in a way that she wouldn't have dared, even hours ago, and to return his kiss with an almost instinctive passion.

'By God, you do love me, after all, you deceiving little minx,' he told her thickly, when they finally drew apart. 'We'll get married as soon as we can arrange it. A big wedding if you like, or a small one, just whatever way you want it to be, my darling.'

'A small one, please, Jacey. Raynor could – could give me away, couldn't he? I'd like it in a church, though.'

'And we'll have Pru for our little attendant, and Trevor will be my best man.'

'Trevor? Is that the doctor? He's really sweet, and I don't even know his other name.'

'Trevor Kendrick. I owe him a lot.'

'So do I,' said Nonie, with a sudden mischievous smile. 'He gave me the courage to come in to see you just now. He said you loved me, and he told me to come in here and cheer you up. If he hadn't been so convincing about it, I don't think I'd have dared. I couldn't believe it.'

'He's been in my confidence for a long time, and of course I've seen him pretty frequently on Raynor's behalf too. He says he wants to get Ray into hospital for some tests tomorrow, but more to confirm what he already knows than because he's worried that he'll slip back at this stage. Where is he now?'

'Raynor? He's with Ilse on the front verandah, I think. Hattie was helping Mrs. Parsons to make up some beds.'

'I'll have to see him after I've had a bit of a nap to get my mind clear. Amongst other things I want to thank him for coming in and helping me out of that hell-hole. When I saw your trunk and all those things you'd been cleaning with Ilse piled up on the side lawn and then looked and saw you weren't with the others, I was so *sure* you were in there—'

'Don't think about it,' Nonie said quickly, sensing the anguish that this line of thought was recapturing.

'No, I'll think about you instead. About *us*. I'm sorry about the house, though, Nonie. It meant a lot to you, didn't it?'

'Only because I'd built up a lot of foolish sentiment around it. Dear old Tuckarimba. It served its purpose by bringing us together, didn't it, and helping Raynor to walk again? I'll always remember it with love and gratitude, but I'm not looking back any more, Jacey. Only forward, to when you and I can be really together, as man and wife.'

'Mrs. J. C. Lomax.' Jacey's hand sought hers. 'Nonie?'

'Yes, Jacey.'

'Nonie, if I were to go to sleep right now, would you still be there when I wake up?'

'Yes, my darling, I'll be here.'

'You're quite sure about that?'

'Quite sure,' she replied softly. 'I'll always be here, for as long as you need me.'

'For a lifetime, then,' said Jacey firmly, and his brown fingers tightened over hers, making quite certain that she would stay right there beside him as he drifted off to sleep.

Have You Missed Any of These
Harlequin Romances?

Have You Missed Any of These
Harlequin Romances?

☐ 1905 TABITHA IN MOONLIGHT,
Betty Neels

☐ 1906 TAKE BACK YOUR LOVE,
Katrina Britt

☐ 1907 ENCHANTMENT IN BLUE,
Flora Kidd

☐ 1908 A TOUCH OF HONEY,
Lucy Gillen

☐ 1909 THE SHIFTING SANDS,
Kay Thorpe

☐ 1910 CANE MUSIC, Joyce Dingwell

☐ 1911 STORMY HARVEST,
Janice Gray

☐ 1912 THE SPANISH INHERITANCE,
Elizabeth Hunter

☐ 1913 THE FLIGHT OF THE HAWK,
Rebecca Stratton

☐ 1914 FLOWERS IN STONY PLACES,
Marjorie Lewty

☐ 1915 EASY TO BARRYVALE,
Yvonne Whittal

☐ 1916 WHEELS OF CONFLICT,
Sue Peters

☐ 1917 ANNA OF STRATHALLAN,
Essie Summers

☐ 1918 THE PLAYER KING,
Elizabeth Ashton

☐ 1919 JUST A NICE GIRL,
Mary Burchell

☐ 1920 HARBOUR OF DECEIT,
Roumelia Lane

☐ 1921 HEAVEN IS GENTLE,
Betty Neels

☐ 1922 COTSWOLD HONEY,
Doris E. Smith

☐ 1923 ALWAYS A RAINBOW,
Gloria Bevan

☐ 1924 THE DARK ISLE,
Mary Wibberley

☐ 1925 BEWARE THE HUNTSMAN,
Sophie Weston

☐ 1926 THE VOICE IN THE
THUNDER, Elizabeth Hunter

☐ 1927 WANDALILLI PRINCESS,
Dorothy Cork

☐ 1928 GENTLE TYRANT, Lucy Gillen

☐ 1929 COLLISION COURSE,
Jane Donnelly

☐ 1930 WEB OF SILVER,
Lucy Gillen

☐ 1931 LULLABY OF LEAVES,
Janice Gray

☐ 1932 THE KISSING GATE,
Joyce Dingwell

☐ 1933 MISS NOBODY FROM
NOWHERE, Elizabeth Ashton

☐ 1934 A STRANGER IS MY LOVE,
Margaret Malcolm

☐ 1935 THAT MAN BRYCE,
Mary Wibberley

☐ 1936 REMEMBERED SERENADE,
Mary Burchell

☐ 1937 HENRIETTA'S OWN CASTLE,
Betty Neels

☐ 1938 SWEET SANCTUARY,
Charlotte Lamb

☐ 1939 THE GIRL AT DANES' DYKE,
Margaret Rome

☐ 1940 THE SYCAMORE SONG,
Elizabeth Hunter

☐ 1941 LOVE AND THE KENTISH
MAID, Betty Beaty

☐ 1942 THE FIRE AND THE FURY,
Rebecca Stratton

☐ 1943 THE GARDEN OF DREAMS,
Sara Craven

☐ 1944 HEART IN THE SUNLIGHT,
Lilian Peake

☐ 1945 THE DESERT CASTLE,
Isobel Chace

☐ 1946 CROWN OF WILLOW,
Elizabeth Ashton

☐ 1947 THE GIRL IN THE BLUE
DRESS, Mary Burchell

☐ 1948 ROSS OF SILVER RIDGE,
Gwen Westwood

☐ 1949 SHINING WANDERER,
Rose Elver

☐ 1950 THE BEACH OF SWEET
RETURNS, Margery Hilton

☐ 1951 RIDE A BLACK HORSE,
Margaret Pargeter

☐ 1952 CORPORATION BOSS,
Joyce Dingwell

All books listed 75c

Have You Missed Any of These
Harlequin Romances?